SOMETHING WAS MOVING ON THE FLOOR, AND CLIVE FELT THE SWEAT OF FEAR ON HIS BODY.

It was a shadow, but not his shadow. It inched forward, its menacing hands upraised like giant claws.

He dared not turn his head to look behind him. He felt a coldness, there was an earthy smell and a dankness as chill as the grave that grew in intensity as the shadow grew closer. So grotesque and distorted was the shadow that it was impossible to tell if a living being cast it . . . .

The
Sin
Eater

and other scientific impossibilities

ELIZABETH WALTER

STEIN AND DAY/*Publishers*/New York

FIRST STEIN AND DAY PAPERBACK EDITION 1984
The Sin Eater was first published in the United States of America in
hardcover by Stein and Day/ *Publishers* in 1968.
Copyright © Elizabeth Walter 1967
All rights reserved, Stein and Day, Incorporated
Printed in the United States of America
STEIN AND DAY/ *Publishers*
Scarborough House
Briarcliff Manor, New York 10510
ISBN 0-8128-8094-3

Contents

The Sin Eater

Although the Reformation destroyed most of the rood-lofts that formerly dignified English parish churches, one or two have survived in out-of-the-way places sufficiently inaccessible to discourage even Puritan zeal: remote Devon fastnesses, or villages and the remains of villages along the Welsh Border, before the real mountains start. One of the best preserved is at Penrhayader, well worth a visit for those who do not mind narrow roads, sharp bends, steep gradients, a trek through the mud of a farmyard, and an abrupt climb to the church. Clive Tomlinson was one who counted these deterrents an attraction. On an October day he arrived at the churchyard gate.

It is not necessary to observe that Clive was interested in old churches. No one came to Penrhayader who was not. It had been a village and was now something less than a hamlet, and what was left of it was half a mile away. In the fourteenth century it had no doubt clustered round the church mound; by the twentieth it had receded—perhaps symbolically. Only the farm, whose stonework looked as old as the church's, remained out of apathy.

Clive, surveying the scene from the churchyard, was not particularly concerned with the how or why. It was typical of his unquestioning, uncomplicated nature, as well-meaning as the printed verse in a Christmas card. Like the card, too, he was a symbol of goodwill towards all men. His life

9

was one perpetual effort to be liked. This had naturally resulted in considerable unpopularity. His late-autumn holiday was being spent alone.

He had hired a small car and set out with no clear idea of where he was going, except that he was heading west. The roads were uncrowded in October; it seemed he could go where he would. Hotels had plenty of accommodation; the whole trip was so easy it was dull. Or perhaps he was bored by shortage of society. In this mood Clive came to Carringford.

Carringford is a county town not a hundred and fifty miles from London, but for all that, decidedly off the map. To the discerning this is its charm, and Clive was intermittently discerning. He surveyed it and decided to stop. The Red Lion was comfortable and quiet, its only other guest as solitary as himself and not disposed to hold long conversations, for he was an archivist at work in the Cathedral Muniment Room.

It was the archivist, Henry Robinson, who alerted Clive to the existence of Penrhayader church, for, finding that the young man was an architectural draughtsman, he mentioned the well-preserved rood-loft. No more was needed to send Clive off on a visit. He excelled at pencil sketches of architectural detail. Some day·he intended to compile a book on *English Church Interiors in the Middle Ages*. Meanwhile he sketched diligently the unusual and the quaint.

Although it was October, the day was as warm as summer. Late bees were buzzing in the hedges, where blackberries glistened and sloes waited to sweeten in the frost. Clive had passed through cider orchards, skirted magnificent tree-clad hills, noted barns piled with hay for the winter and clamps of turnips, mangolds and swedes. But as he approached the Welsh Border and its bleak hill-slopes terraced with sheep-runs, the farmer's lot by comparison was poor. When he had picked his way through the farm below the church at Penrhayader, no one had even come curiously to the door. No dog had barked, no cattle had lowed, all was silent; it seemed a house of the dead, especially since the windows were shut tight and curtained, as though the inhabitants were still in bed.

Yet though neglected, the farm was by no means abandoned. A few fowls scratched in the dirt; a pig could be smelt if not inspected; a cat squinted from the window-sill. Only the human inhabitants were missing, and they, perhaps, had merely withdrawn. As he passed, Clive could have sworn he saw a curtain twitch at a window, as though someone upstairs peered out.

Reflecting that country people were often shy of strangers, Clive strode energetically on his way. He was unimaginative and not inclined to introspection. What might have struck another as strange or sinister was to him without significance.

It was after two when he descended from the church mound. The rood-loft was the finest he had seen. A series of sketches reposed in his portfolio. He looked forward to showing them to Mr Robinson when he got in.

It was as he was picking his way through the farmyard, where the mud and filth and ooze were ankle-deep, that a voice behind him, croaking and sepulchral, enunciated the word 'Afternoon'.

Clive turned. The door of the farmhouse had opened and an old man stood blinking in the light, like some diurnally-awakened creature of darkness, unable to understand why it is not night.

'Good afternoon,' Clive responded. His greeting lacked its usual warmth. He had taken quick stock of the farmer, and was not attracted by what he saw.

The old man seemed unaware of it. Clive reflected that country people could be very obtuse. Surely the old man did not suppose he wished to linger in conversation in this unsavoury spot?

The old man, however, appeared to have just that notion. 'Fine day,' he observed, not looking at the sky.

'Wonderful for October,' Clive returned. His voice was breathless as his foot slipped and he skidded in the mud.

The old man stood back and held the door open. 'Will you come in a bit?' he enquired.

'It's very good of you, but—no, thank you.' Clive felt increasingly the urge to get away.

' 'Twouldn't be for long,' the old man hastened to assure him. 'Just long enough to see my son.'

Clive had no desire to extend acquaintance to the next generation. 'I'm sorry,' he called. 'I can't wait.'

He made his way across the rest of the farmyard and began fumbling at the gate. It was a heavy five-barred one, fastened by the usual peg and chain. He had opened it easily enough, but now, encumbered by his portfolio and its contents, which he was afraid of dropping in the mud, he found the peg apparently jammed in its chain-link.

The old man watched him from the doorway, but made no move to help. He was short and stocky, with a paunch and a face at once sly and open—shrewd eyes and a toothless idiot mouth. He was dressed in a pair of stained and faded corduroy trousers maintained in place by a belt and a piece of string, and a shirt of indeterminate colour which revealed at the neck an edge of greyish vest. His coat was frayed at the cuffs, its buttons off or hanging, and, like his cheeks, his jowls, and his paunch, its pockets sagged.

Clive struggled again with the gate-pin but could not shift it, although nothing held it that he could see. There was no help for it: he would have to climb over, for the old man obviously was not coming to his aid.

He placed one foot on the bottom bar, tucked his port-folio under his arm more securely, and prepared to swing astride, when the mud on his shoes made his foot slip, the portfolio jerked and two of his best sketches fluttered down. With an exclamation of annoyance Clive turned to retrieve them, but the old man had got there first. He had seized the larger and nearer drawing, and was making off with it towards the house.

'Hi!' Clive called, 'where are you going?'

' 'Twill dry off better in the house. And you can't put it away all muddy. You'd best come in, I reckon, and dry yourself.'

There was some sense in the suggestion. Clive reluctantly followed the old man. His shoes and trouser-bottoms were stiff with mud. Besides he wanted his drawing. If only the place were clean! He had already noted with horror the single tap in the farmyard, the absence of telephone wires, the suspect shack within easy reach of the back door, the cobwebs round the window-frames. The farmhouse, built of stone with a low-pitched slate roof, was unbelievably primitive. Its four small windows barely broke the wall's solid surface; they were not far removed from arrow-slits. Clive could imagine someone holding out in it as in a beleaguered fortress, and the picture did not comfort him. The combination of isolation, neglect, primitive conditions and his own instinctive repugnance to entering the house or having anything to do with its inhabitants added up to something overwhelmingly grim.

He was unprepared for the heat of the living-room as they entered. Despite the warmth of the day, a fire glowed red in the grate. On top of it a black kettle sputtered. A gridiron leaned against the hearth. All cooking, Clive realized, was done on this fire or in the oven built into the wall beside it. There was no sink, though an enamel bowl stood on the table. Slops and scraps were presumably emptied outside. The ceiling was low and blackened by the smoke from the fire, from candles and a paraffin lamp. The floor was stone, uneven but not unswept, Clive noted. One wall showed patches of damp. In the corner a staircase rose steeply; from the room above came the sound of a shuffling tread. The old man went straight to the foot of the stairs and called softly, 'Mother!'

'What is it?' came a voice overhead.

'I've brought a young man to see Eddie.'

The voice came to the head of the stairs. 'Didn't I tell you someone would be coming? Have faith, Evan Preece, have faith.'

'Ay, you were right. You're always right, Becky. Tell me now, are you ready yet?'

'Not far off. Ask the gentleman to sit down a minute. He'll be glad to dry by the fire if his feet are wet.'

The old man turned to Clive apologetically, 'She'll not be long, but 'tis a woman's business, see. Sit you down until it's time to go up to Eddie.'

'I'm afraid,' Clive began, 'I can't stay.'

'You can stay long enough to see my son,' the old man insisted. ' 'Tis the only visitor he'll have. You were sent so that Eddie should lie easy and us have an answer to our prayers.'

In spite of himself, Clive found this solicitude for a sick son touching. Within their limits, they obviously gave him every care. And if one were bedridden in this outpost one might go from one year's end to the other without setting eyes on a fresh face. No wonder they were anxious for Eddie to have a visitor; it was an event they would talk about for weeks. It would be churlish to refuse this small act of kindness. Was not one enjoined to visit the sick?

He rescued his drawings from the old man, put them back in his portfolio and was tying the tapes when a creaking from the corner made him look round; the old woman was coming down the stairs.

She was smaller, frailer, greyer than her husband, her back bowed in what was almost a hump. She wore a cross-over print overall on top of her garments, black stockings and bedroom slippers on her feet. She had brown bluish-filmed eyes, moist with rheum or with crying, and she greeted Clive deferentially.

'Would you like to come up, sir?' she invited. 'It's all ready for you up there now.'

In the background the old man was hurrhing and hawking and trying to catch her eye.

'Did you put the wine out, Becky?' he asked at last in desperation.

The old woman nodded. 'With the plate on top of it like you said.'

The old man seemed satisfied. 'We'd best go up. Lead the way, Becky.' He closed in, bringing up the rear. Clive had no option but to pick his way up the steep, narrow staircase which opened directly into the upper room.

The curtains drawn across the small window shrouded everything in a curious daylight gloom, making the low room seem larger and mysterious, although it was ordinary enough. The floor sloped so sharply that a chest of drawers near the window appeared to be tilted on edge, but except for a high-backed upright chair in the corner, most of the space was occupied by an old-fashioned brass-knobbed bed. On the bed a man of indeterminate age was lying, grey-haired but by no means old. His face was sunken, and the deep grooves from nose to chin had not yet smoothed out. His hands were folded and his eyes were closed.

It was so unexpected that Clive, who had never been in the presence of the dead until now, was tempted to turn and run, but the old people were standing as if on guard at the head of the steep stairs. There was nothing for it but to go on as he had begun. Besides, his instinct had been ridiculous. There was nothing to fear from the dead. The still figure—how wasted it was!—could not hurt him. He took a cautious step nearer the bed.

All the time one level of his mind was working frantically in search of something suitable to say. He was not even sure why he had been invited into the death-chamber, nor what response was expected or desired.

'I'm awfully sorry,' he said tritely. 'It must be very hard to lose a son.'

'Ay.' The old man nodded in agreement.

The old woman dabbed at her eyes. 'Cruel it is, and him not forty.' She added inconsequentially, 'He was our only one.'

The revelation of the dead man's age shook Clive considerably. He had taken him for fifty at least.

'Had he been ill long?' he asked, although he guessed the answer.

'About two year. Ever since they let him come home.'

Clive wondered if this meant that the dead man had been of unsound mind as well as consumptive. The parents struck him as being decidedly odd. They seemed to hover, waiting for something. He had obviously failed to find the right remark. Did the old woman expect compliments on her handiwork; 'How beautifully you have laid him out'; or the old man seek to have their family resemblance noted, for it was evident that they had been much alike?

His glance strayed towards the aperture in the wall near the bed-head where, quite obviously, there once had been a door. The old man followed his gaze and hastened to offer explanation.

'Couldn't bear to sleep in the back after what had happened, Eddie couldn't. Said he'd rather sleep in the mud of the yard outside.' His voice faltered; then he went on more strongly: 'So Mother and I had to let him have our room. 'Twas a bit awkward-like, but we'd have done more than that for Eddie. I took the door off its hinges because it squeaked. It opened inwards, you see; it were heavy for Mother to pull it; and we were afraid of waking Eddie with the noise.'

'He slept so lightly,' the old woman said in amplification. She turned away to wipe the tears from her eyes.

' "One shall be taken," ' Clive observed sententiously in what he hoped was an appropriate tone of voice.

To his consternation, this remark which he had thought quite suitable, appeared to upset the old woman very much. Her eyes filled with tears and her mouth trembled. It seemed that her whole body shook. Her husband laid a broken-nailed hand on her shoulder—a gesture of warning as much as of sympathy—but she shook it off and turned to face Clive in defiance, as though he had insulted her personally.

'Yes, one shall be taken,' she cried, 'and that the wrong 'un. My son didn't deserve to suffer as he did. I told 'em that, for the wench was nowt but a wanton and there's others to blame as well as him.'

'Becky, Becky——' the old man began in protest, but she turned on him. 'Hold your tongue, Evan Preece! Why should your own son suffer when there's another more guilty? You know right enough who I mean.'

'Ay, I know.' The old man sighed heavily. 'But 'tis the way of things, Becky, see. That other was—well, who he was,' he concluded.

'He's a——'

He raised his hand threateningly. 'Shut your mouth!' There was no mistaking his menace. He was suddenly the stronger of the two. The old woman cowered and mumbled, but was careful to keep her words indistinct.

'Now, sir—' the old man turned to Clive as if nothing had happened—'you must take a glass of wine with my son.'

For a moment Clive thought he had misheard him, but the old man was already moving to the foot of the bed, where, Clive now noticed, a small table covered with a clean white cloth was standing, and on it a jug and a plate. The plate, posed upon the jug, contained a small round drop-scone, something like a currantless Welsh cake, and no doubt cooked on the gridiron Clive had noticed in the living-room. The jug contained a blackish wine.

As Clive watched, the old man filled a wine-glass. There was only one glass and one plate. Refreshment was to be offered solely to the stranger. It was hardly a sociable meal.

And partaken of in the presence of a corpse, too! Clive backed away and violently shook his head. 'No, really! Excuse me, but I couldn't. Not—not with your son lying there upon the bed.'

'But you *must* drink,' the old man exclaimed, 'else he'll never lie easy. You must eat and drink to save him from his sins.'

' 'Tis the last of my blackberry wine,' the old woman quaveringly insisted. 'I've been saving it for such a day as this.'

'Won't you—won't you join me, then?' Clive suggested. As one, the old people shook their heads.

'Drink and eat,' the old man commanded, holding glass and plate outstretched across the corpse. 'And may all thy sins be forgiven thee,' he added.

The old woman's assent sounded like amen.

Clive sipped the wine and took a mouthful of the round cake. The wine was syrupy and very strong. The cake crumbled to a paste which he forced himself to swallow. It felt as though it were sticking to his tongue. His companions —two living and one dead—were still and silent. Only the old man's breathing sounded loud, and—to Clive—the movement of his own jaws and the constrictions of his throat as he swallowed, watched all the time by the old woman at the head of the stairs.

Clive had read about wakes and thought they sounded jolly in a macabre way, but this was like no wake he had ever known. It was more like some communion rite. Some mystic rapport between himself and the dead man. His sense of uneasiness increased. He could see no reason to refuse the refreshment offered; besides, he did not wish to offend, but he wished profoundly that he had not been prevailed on to accept it. As he gulped down the last of the wine and the round cake, his gorge rose until he feared he would vomit on the spot. It was as though his stomach itself was rejecting what it had been offered.

He turned to the old woman. 'I must go.'

Silently she stood aside to allow him passage; silently she followed him down the stairs; silently she watched as he gathered his portfolio together and turned towards the outer door. Then, suddenly, she was on her knees before him, catching at his hand, kissing it with her withered lips. 'Thank you for what you've done! A blessing on you for what you've lifted from the soul of my poor boy!'

'Becky!' Her husband's voice sounded angrily as he reached the foot of the stairs behind her. 'Let the gentleman alone and none of your carryings-on. 'Tis a miracle that he came, right enough, but we must let him go now—far away from us and our innocent son.'

'Yes, innocent!' The old woman's voice rose sharply in a strange, triumphant cry. Her husband opened the outer door and Clive passed through it.

Not one of them attempted a goodbye.

Unfortunately Mr Robinson was not in to dinner that evening, and Clive, his portfolio beside him, had to nurse his disappointment through three courses and prepare himself for an evening's solitude. He was therefore quite ready to be sociable when Barnabas Elms joined him in the lounge.

Barnabas Elms was well known in Carringford, though it could not be said he was well liked. He was a bachelor, a bore and a busybody. Graver charges were hinted at, also beginning with a 'b'. He was present at many civic occasions in his capacity as a councillor, but was seldom welcome at any of these, partly because he had appointed himself a standing one-man watch committee to ensure that what he called 'decent people's feelings' were not outraged. It was Barnabas who rooted out 'dirty' books from the Public Library, returning them with the words objected to underlined. It was Barnabas who insisted that shop-window dummies should be discreetly veiled in dust-sheets in the intervals while their clothes were being changed. It was Barnabas who had objected to a nude by a well-known sculptor being erected in the Town Hall Square. Barnabas, in short, who upheld Carringford's reputation for being in the rear of progress and counted this a source of pride.

Having no friends, Barnabas was forced to fall back on the company of his relations, and he had rather few of those. But the wife of the proprietor of the Red Lion was his cousin, and he was in the habit of dropping in. If, as often happened, there were visitors, he would eagerly introduce himself. Since he was a member of the licensing committee, his visitations had to be endured.

Tonight it was Clive's misfortune to endure him. Even Clive found Barnabas difficult to like. He was about to give up trying and withdraw bedwards, when Mr Robinson arrived. Mr Robinson had had an excellent dinner with one of the canons in the Close. He had also deciphered a particularly illegible fourteenth-century document and his mood was such that he was prepared to be tolerant of anyone, even of Barnabas, whom he had already met and disliked. Not for a long time had Barnabas been welcomed with so much cordiality. He concluded that here at last was a sympathetic ear, and immediately launched into a denunciation of Carringford's latest offence against decency: the toleration of a coloured family on a council housing estate.

Unfortunately—from Barnabas's point of view—there had been no trouble.

'It's scandalous,' he complained, despairing of the folly of his fellow citizens. 'People will accept anything today. In ten years' time we shan't be able to recognize this city.'

'I wonder. Its citizens have some pretty permanent characteristics,' Mr Robinson observed. 'In the fourteenth century—or so I have been reading—they confiscated the property of those who traded or visited with the Jews.'

'Who's talking about the Jews?' Barnabas demanded.

Mr Robinson gave a long, exaggerated sigh.

Clive interposed, anxious to smooth things over: 'I went to Penrhayader today.'

Mr Robinson immediately looked interested.

'You pick the rummest places,' Barnabas objected. 'What's at Penrhayader, I'd like to know?'

'A rood-loft in the church.' Clive produced his sketches.

'What's a rood-loft?' Barnabas asked.

Clive did his best to explain, while Mr Robinson examined the drawings, and made gratifyingly appreciative noises, looking up at last to ask, 'What's the place like?'

Clive described it as best he could.

'I ask only because I've come across the name in old documents. In the seventeenth century the Puritans classified it as a hotbed of Popery.'

'I'm not surprised. It is a very remote village. Old customs have undoubtedly lingered on. I experienced an instance of that while I was there this morning.'

'I don't know about old customs,' Barnabas interrupted, 'but there've been some shocking goings-on there in recent times.'

Clive was determined not to be denied his story. 'As I was

passing the farm by the church—it's very isolated,' he continued, 'an old man came out and insisted I go in to see his son.'

'What did his son want with you?' Barnabas demanded.

'Nothing. When I went in I found that he was dead.'

'Perhaps they mistook you for the doctor?' Mr Robinson suggested.

'No—' Clive shook his head—'they simply wanted me to go in and drink their son's health.'

'Drink his health!'

'That's what it seemed like. They insisted I must drink a glass of wine and eat a little cake, with this man laid out on the bed before me. It was all I could do to get it down.'

'You mean you had to eat and drink in the presence of the corpse?' Mr Robinson asked, his eyes staring.

'Yes, and very unnerving it was.'

'Could you describe what you ate? Did they say anything to you?'

'I had a glass of blackberry wine and a sort of small, flat, currantless Welsh cake.'

Mr Robinson exhaled very softly. 'The genuine articles, no less. And the people—what were they like? Did they give any explanation?'

'Not that I remember,' Clive said. 'They were very old, very frail, I should think illiterate——'

Mr Robinson nodded.

'They didn't eat or drink themselves,' Clive remembered, 'but they seemed terribly grateful that I did. The old man said something about making his son lie easy. I had to eat and drink to save him from his sins.'

Mr Robinson folded his hands in a reverent gesture. 'To think the practice still continues!' he exclaimed.

'What practice?' Clive asked, uneasy and bewildered.

'The custom of sin-eating for the dead. It is peculiar to the Welsh Border and is symbolized by the taking of bread and wine in the presence of the corpse.'

'And what was the point of it?'

'It was believed that the dead man's sins would be transferred to the account of whoever ate and drank in his presence, thus enabling him to sleep till Judgment Day, provided only that the bread and wine were handed across the body.'

Clive laughed nervously. 'I took on more than I knew. But why didn't the old people eat and drink to ensure the poor fellow slept easy? He was their son, after all.'

'Because the sin-eater must be a stranger, preferably someone who comes from far away, so that when he goes he will take the dead man's sins with him, away from the community in which he lived.'

'Like the Israelites driving forth the scapegoat.'

'Yes, the two ideas may very possibly be linked. What fascinates me is that sin-eating still survives. It was last recorded in the mid-nineteenth century.'

'My grandfather knew of it,' Barnabas said suddenly. 'I've heard him say he was asked to sin-eat for some man in an outlying village, but he knew what he was doing and refused.'

'Should I have refused?' Clive asked. 'They seemed so anxious.'

'Ah—' Barnabas paused dramatically—'anxious is just what those old folk would be.'

'Why they more than any others?'

Barnabas did not answer at first. Then: 'Their name's Preece, isn't it?'

'I believe it is,' Clive replied.

'And their son's name was Edward?'

Clive nodded.

'Then I wouldn't want to be in your shoes.'

'Why? Was Edward Preece particularly sinful?'

'He was a murderer,' Barnabas said.

A few days later Clive returned to London, having cut short his stay in Carringford. The sin-eating episode had upset him, although he could not quite say why. On the face of it, it seemed absurd to bother about some ancient pagan superstition surviving by a fluke from the past. Sin could not be transferred; it was against the Christian religion. It was also against common sense.

Nevertheless, the thought recurred to him constantly that he now had murder to his account. He was a murderer and no one knew it—a man who went unpunished and un-hanged. Not that the original committer of the crime had been hanged either; he had merely been imprisoned for life, or more exactly for twelve years. 'Twelve years,' Barnabas Elms had exclaimed, 'that's all they gave him! Twelve years for murdering his wife!'

Clive was by now familiar with Preece's story, which Barnabas had needed no persuading to tell. It was evidently one which had made a deep impression upon him. He told it unexpectedly well.

Edward Preece had married his childhood sweetheart, a girl from a neighbouring farm. Elsie had been young and very pretty. Barnabas chronicled her charms. Unfortunately life with Edward and his bigoted parents had proved too narrow for the young wife's happiness. Twice in the first year she ran away and sought refuge with her own people, and twice she returned because of Edward's distress. For Edward loved Elsie to distraction; the world would have been too paltry to lay at her feet. 'He spoiled her,' Barnabas observed, with the subdued satisfaction of one who has successfully prophesied catastrophe. 'He made her feel there was nothing too good for her, so naturally she got to thinking she could do no wrong. And when she found a catch like Dick Roper was after her, she didn't bother to resist for long.'

Dick Roper was the only son of the local landowner, an arrogant, swaggering young dandy who had already caused his father trouble enough. Most of the trouble was over women—Barnabas gave details—for whom his appetite was vast. He had done his military service as a commando and then enrolled in an agricultural college, but he had been sent down because of some scandal, and his father was now keeping him on a tight rein, making him live at home, work hard at farming, and take his part in running the estate. Bored, sulky and resentful, Dick met Elsie. When next he stopped to think, it was too late.

Barnabas had been loud in his condemnation of Elsie, but Mr Robinson enquired: 'Don't you think young Roper was more to blame? He seduced her, from what you've told us.'

'Mr Roper—Sir Richard I should say now—is a gentleman.'

'But he seduced the wife of one of his own—or his father's —tenants. I don't call that a gentlemanly act.'

'Boys will be boys,' Barnabas said with an attempt at lightness.

'And girls will be girls, no doubt. What happened? Did Elsie find she was pregnant?'

'What happened was that Edward Preece found out.'

'What did he do?' Clive asked, with apprehension.

'Ah, you may well ask that! It seems the husband was like they say—the last to know—and when he heard, he didn't believe it. He resolved to keep a watch, fooled Elsie into thinking he had gone ploughing, and then crept back towards the house. At the trial he claimed he saw a man cross the farmyard, but from that distance could not recognize who he was. Believing he would catch his wife red-handed, he burst in on her—and found her dead.'

'It doesn't sound very likely,' Clive objected.

'No. The jury threw it out. For Dick Roper testified that he arrived a quarter of an hour later to find Preece with his hands round Elsie's throat. She had been strangled—there were bruises—and Preece was a violent-tempered man. He had cause for anger—Roper admitted it. What more natural than that he went a bit too far? It is easy to sin.' Barnabas sounded as if he had just discovered it.

Mr Robinson turned on him. 'Shouldn't that be a challenge, instead of being put forward as an excuse?'

Barnabas said, smiling smugly, 'It is not for us to judge.'

'And what became of Roper?' Mr Robinson enquired grimly.

'He went to Australia. He has a sheep farm in New South Wales. Doing well, too. He decided to stay on out there even after his father died.' Barnabas shook his head over this dereliction of duty.

'What about the old people?' Clive asked suddenly. 'Where were they while Elsie was being killed?'

'They were out. They claimed they knew nothing.'

'And the jury accepted that?'

Barnabas shrugged. 'Personally, I'm convinced the Preeces knew something. The old woman certainly did. She tried her best to pin the crime on Dick Roper. But she was too partisan—the judge directed the jury to disregard her.'

I can understand that, Clive thought. She'd count each breath Eddie drew, the hairs on his head would be numbered, if his heart so much as faltered she would know. He felt again her withered lips against his fingers, the senile trembling of her toothless jaws. She and her husband had continued to live on that farm where their daughter-in-law had been murdered, to sleep in the very room where she had died. 'The wench was nowt but a wanton,' Mrs Preece had protested. 'My son did not deserve to suffer when there was others as much to blame.'

As in some old ballad where emotions are not explicitly stated, her words were remarkable for what they did not say. Elsie had found life narrow and difficult with her in-laws. Twice in that first year of marriage she had rebelled and run away. It was easy to imagine the unforgiving resentment with which her return would be eyed. She had come back in response to Edward's pleadings, but the old people would sooner far that she had died.

And when she took up with Dick Roper—surely her mother-in-law would be the first to know. Was it she who had told Edward that his wife was no longer faithful, hoping thus to deal his love a death-blow?

There was no limit to the speculations one could indulge in. A thousand questions sprang to mind, destined one and all to remain unanswered. Clive wondered if their urgency would ever recede. For whether he liked it or not, he was now a part of this tragic situation: he bore the guilt though he had not done the deed.

This thought accompanied Clive back to London and was

with him in daily life—in his work in the architect's office, in crowded tube-trains, in his bed at nights. He did not discuss his guilt for fear of ridicule. The whole story sounded far-fetched. Who had ever heard of sin-eating? And if he had, who would believe in it? Clive assured himself repeatedly that nothing had been altered by his consumption of that tainted wine and bread. In vain. Now that he knew the significance of his actions he felt inextricably bound to the dead.

It was some such powerful but ill-formulated notion that led him to return to Carringford. The following autumn found him again at the Red Lion, where Barnabas Elms, who called by what he termed coincidence on Clive's first evening, inspected the young man with an air of mournful anticipation, like an undertaker visiting a sick friend.

'Returning to the scene of the crime?' he enquired archly.

'I don't know. I hadn't thought of it.'

Clive was astonished to hear himself lie so fluently. He had thought of nothing but Penrhayader all the way down. It was absurd, of course, and there would be no sequel to his longing—but he wanted to see the place again.

'The old folks are in the churchyard,' Barnabas informed him. 'Died last winter. There was no sin-eating for *them*. She went first and he followed. You'll be able to poke around the place in peace.'

'I have no intention of doing so,' Clive said unconvincingly.

Barnabas shook his head and solemnly closed one eye.

The next day brought a perfect autumn morning, laced with spiders' webs and mist and dew. Clive resolved to delay his visit to Penrhayader no longer, and after breakfast he set out. The drive passed without incident, and, off the main road, there was little traffic about. Within an hour he was turning down the lane leading to church and farmyard, so overgrown that it was almost lost. A robin singing cheerfully in the hedgerow fell silent as he approached. A blackberry trail, bent by the passage of some vehicle, freed itself and sprang back viciously. He noticed then that the hedges on either side of the lane were damaged, as though a visitor had only recently passed. Some other enthusiast to see the rood-loft in the church, perhaps, or a possible buyer for the farm.

Despite this, he almost failed to notice the car when he came upon it, so carefully was it concealed, backed out of sight into a gateway where the hedge was a profusion of blackberry and old man's beard. Clive wondered at the choice of parking place since there was open ground near the farm, but decided the driver must be unfamiliar with his surroundings and had stopped at the first suitable spot.

Clive had no wish to encounter the owner, but the farm-yard looked empty enough. He had thought it desolate when he first visited it a year ago, but that was nothing to how it looked today. The peg-and-chain fastening on the gate had rusted. Once again he was obliged to climb. The mire underfoot had dried—from disuse rather than drought, he suspected—and it was possible now to see that the farm-yard was paved with flags. But the chickens had vanished; the pig could no longer be smelt; and the door of the lean-to shack near the back porch swung open, revealing the earth-closet for what it was.

As Clive came round the side of the farmhouse, he received a further shock. The downstairs windows were broken and boarded; two planks nailed crosswise barred the door. It looked like a travesty of the plague sign; almost he expected to hear the cry, 'Bring out your dead!' Instead the silence was absolute; even the upland wind had dropped. The decay around him seemed that of centuries; he could not believe it was the work of a single year—of a twelvemonth, he thought, reckoning back to his last visit; a twelvemonth and a day.

The coincidence shook him for no logical reason. It was absurd to be affected by a ballad-monger's trite phrase. What if it was the length of time for which fairies were said to bewitch a man, the span between burial and first walking of the ghost? No one believed such nonsense in the twentieth century. He continued resolutely on his way.

It was as he was passing the far side of the house on his tour of inspection that something prompted Clive to look round. The single sash-window on this side was neither broken nor boarded, and a man was climbing out. The window was at ground-level and opened into a dairy. As Clive watched, the man dropped lightly to the ground. He was well-dressed, well-built, but rather stocky. His head was bowed to show dark hair thinning on the top but arranged carefully and expensively. Clive could not see his face.

As though aware of being scrutinized, the man looked up suddenly. Clive noted sun-tanned skin and brown eyes regarding him suspiciously, even while the man politely said 'Good afternoon.'

Clive returned the greeting, adding, 'What are you doing here?'

'Having a look round.' The voice was twangy and unpleasing.

'Are you a prospective purchaser?'

The man laughed silently. 'Are you an agent?'

Clive disclaimed all agency connections with such conviction that the intruder almost relaxed. He volunteered a little information: he had known the Preeces once, long ago.

'So did I,' Clive said automatically.

'But you're not from these parts.'

The stranger rapped it out so smartly that Clive was uncertain what to say. 'I'm a visitor here,' he offered.

'So am I.' The stranger seemed satisfied. Abruptly he switched to something else. 'This place has gone to rack and ruin. It's changed a lot since the last time I stood here.'

'When was that?' Clive asked with curiosity.

'Years ago.' The man seemed about to say more, but refrained. Instead he returned to the farm. 'I hear the old folks died only last winter. It must have been in a bad state long before then.'

'Oh, it was,' Clive assured him. 'When I saw it last year I thought no one lived here. But of course they were old and their son obviously hadn't been able to do much——'

The stranger interrupted him: 'Do you mean to say you knew Eddie Preece?'

Clive hesitated. Should he tell him? 'I didn't know him well,' he temporized.

'How long did you know him?' the stranger demanded.

'Not long.' Clive was carefully vague. He was beginning to resent the examination. What right had this intruder to question him?

The intruder, however, was unaware of Clive's resentment. Indeed, he seemed unaware of Clive. 'Then you didn't know him before,' he murmured.

Clive asked very deliberately: 'Do you mean before he murdered his wife?'

'So you know!' The stranger seemed almost relieved by this discovery, as though he could speak more freely now. Then an instant later: 'How do you know?' he asked quickly. 'You said you didn't come from these parts.'

'It's no secret,' Clive responded. 'I heard about it when I was down last year.'

'A bad business,' the stranger commented. 'Eddie Preece didn't deserve to suffer like that.'

There was so much sorrow in his voice that Clive was moved by it. This man must have known Preece well—a school friend, perhaps. They must be about the same age, he decided, trying to cast his mind back to the dead man lying on the bed.

'Why are you here?' he asked again.

'I thought it would be—interesting.' The man lingered over the word, as though it had some secret significance. 'I like to revisit old haunts.'

He smiled then, showing all his teeth in a shark's grin, and added: 'Though I should have preferred to be alone.'

Clive realized that he disliked this arrogant stranger. 'When I saw you, you seemed to be breaking in.'

'I was, but there's nothing worth the taking.'

'Are you telling me the furniture's still there?'

'It has to rot somewhere, and there's no point in taking it away—it might as well stay here. Since Eddie Preece died first, there's no heir.'

'Eddie Preece died a year ago yesterday.'

'So you know that too! You seem to be very well informed. But I assure you, I didn't come here to steal, if that's what you're thinking. I've touched nothing. Come in and see for yourself.'

With one hand the stranger thrust the sash-window upwards and stood back for Clive to go first. Once again, Clive felt himself outmanœuvred. Who was this man to do the honours of the house?

He stood resolutely still. 'I'll take your word for it.'

'Don't do that.' The stranger's laugh had an unpleasant sound.

Clive turned on his heel.

'Stay!' the other man called after him. 'I can show you something interesting inside.'

Curiosity is a powerful human motive. In Clive it was particularly strong. He hesitated, and the stranger beckoned imperiously. 'It's quite safe, if that's what's worrying you, and I promise I shan't keep you long.'

Thoughts of hidden treasure or secret cupboards lured Clive, for what else could the house contain? Reluctantly he put one foot over the sill of the dairy window. As he did so, he was seized by a feeling of horror that he could neither combat nor satisfactorily explain.

The dairy was chill and vault-like. Its window darkened as the stranger clambered in. Instinctively Clive sought to put a distance between them. For some reason this man affected him unpleasantly.

The dairy opened into the kitchen, which was much as Clive remembered it, though hung with cobwebs now and made gloomy by the boarded windows. There were ashes still in the hearth. The place stank of mice and damp and mildew. Their footsteps rang loudly on the stone floor.

In the corner the staircase ascended, steep and narrow, to the room of death above. Clive led the way and the other followed. At the top he stood blocking the escape. Just so had the old couple stood, Clive remembered, and now they, like their son, were dead. There had been no sin-eating for them, Barnabas Elms had told him. He hoped they lay easy, even so.

It was as he stood in the middle of the room with his back to the window that he thought he heard the sound. A board creaked, as boards do in old houses, but there was something more besides. Without knowing exactly how he knew it, Clive became aware that there was someone in the room next door. It seemed impossible. He glanced at his companion to see if he had heard it. The man was standing rigid, a look of terror on his face. His eyes were fixed, the whites suddenly very prominent, on the open space where once had been the bedroom door.

Clive followed his gaze. At first he noticed nothing. From where he stood no one was visible. He was about to move to the head of the stairs to join the stranger, when his eye was caught by something on the floor. It lay, long and black, stretching out from the empty doorway, unnaturally elongated and—Clive could have sworn—unnaturally dark. Though the light was not strong, the outline was unmistakable. It was the shadow of a man, unmoving, stark.

And not only of a man. The man had a companion, whom he was grasping, in fear or anger, by the throat. It was a woman—Clive could see her long hair streaming backwards, and—quite clearly—the outline of her breast. The shadows were as still as if of statues. Not even the woman's hair stirred. Apart from their elongation caused by the light's angle, no single detail was blurred.

Clive stood still for so long that he wondered if he too had become a statue—until he heard himself gasping for breath. Or was it the stranger who was gasping? Even across the room, Clive could see that his chest heaved. He was clutching the newel-post at the stairhead. From his colour and posture Clive judged he was about to faint. He glanced again at the shadows. They lay exactly as before. Whatever it was in the next room that cast them, he had to see what lay beyond that missing door.

In three quick strides Clive crossed to where the stranger was standing and gripped him firmly by the arm.

'It's all right. Take it easy. There are two of us. Whoever they are, they won't do us any harm.'

He was not certain of this; hence his insistence on equal numbers. His companion relaxed slightly as he spoke.

'Did you see them too? Then they *were* there. I thought I was dreaming. But now, thank heaven, they've gone.'

Clive looked and found the next-door room devoid of occupants, or at least that part of it which he could see. He looked at the floor, but the long black shadows had vanished.

'We must have been imagining things,' he said.

He knew in his heart that he had imagined nothing, but it was all he could think of to say. He hoped that the stranger would seize upon it. Between them, they would chase these shadows away. And Clive, at least, longed for such reassurance, for without it, what was it that had been in the room next door?

To his dismay, however, the stranger did not seize on his explanations. Instead he said: 'We imagined nothing. It was Eddie and Elsie in there. He was standing at the foot of the bed and he had his hands round her throat just like I saw them. Do you think I'll ever forget a sight like that?'

Clive said, without surprise, 'You're Richard Roper.'

The other nodded impatiently. 'Hadn't you guessed?'

Clive knew now that he had guessed; that he had known from the moment he saw him that this was the man responsible for Elsie Preece's death; and therefore the man responsible for the sin he, Clive, now carried.

'I thought you were in Australia,' he said.

'So I am—was—until a week ago. Then I decided to come home.'

'Why?'

'I don't know. It's only for a short visit. I flew in to London last night, hired a car, and drove straight down here. I wanted to see it *that* bad.' Roper snapped his fingers like a man clinching an argument. 'Funny how things get you, isn't it?'

He stood there, so sure of himself, so debonair and smiling, even though his face was still blanched with fear, that Clive felt himself choke with rage—an unfamiliar sensation, for his temper was normally cool.

Nevertheless, he managed to master it, and replied, 'You seem to have got more than you bargained for.'

'You're dead right,' Roper said.

'Did you see what you actually saw on that day when . . . when . . .'

'Exactly the same.' Roper indicated the stairs behind him. 'I came up there. The house was very still. As I crossed the yard, I had heard Elsie crying out and I was frightened. I had thought she was alone in the house.' He grinned suddenly. 'Everyone will have told you we were lovers. It was what lent lustre to the case. I used to wait till the Preeces were out and then go and see her. Sometimes we'd meet out, but it was difficult for her to get away.'

'But they were out that afternoon?'

'Yes, all of them. The old man had gone into town. The old woman was down in the village. Eddie had ploughing to do. I watched them all set off after mid-day dinner. Eddie was the last to leave. Elsie waved him off from the door— that was our signal. I knew then that the coast was clear for me.

'It takes about a quarter of an hour from the point where I was watching to get to the Preeces' house. As I crossed the yard, I told you I heard Elsie screaming. I wondered then if Eddie had come back. The screams stopped when I was half-way across the farmyard. There was a trail of mud over the kitchen floor. It looked as though Eddie had returned unexpectedly. I went upstairs two at a time. As I reached the head of the stairs, I turned and saw them. They were like statues, and Eddie had her by the throat. She was half undressed, and her clothes were slipping off her shoulders. Her long dark hair had come loose and was hanging down. Her head was limp and lolling sideways. Eddie looked like a man in a trance. I don't believe he knew what he'd done to her—I told them that at the trial. I said, "My God, you've killed her!" and he looked at me and shook his head—slowly, like a bull that's bewildered. Then he let go of her and fell sobbing on the bed.'

Clive listened. The story had a horrible coherence. It also had the glibness of one told many times. He could picture Roper, a little drunk, talking to reporters and pub acquaintances. His dislike of the man increased. He also found him slightly sinister, in a well-dressed, snake-like way. Roper's eyes, small, bright and unblinking, assessed his every reaction with an intentness that Clive found strange.

And yet not strange, for there was something wrong with the story, and Roper watched to see if this time his bluff would be called. But it never had been, and Eddie Preece had been convicted. Why after all these years should his confidence suddenly fail? Was it the apparition of the two figures that had shaken him, and the memories they conjured up? Or was it simply that he was out of practice? He could not have told his tale for many years.

Clive looked away from him towards the bedroom, empty and rotting like everything else in the house. From the stairhead he could see clearly where the two figures must have been standing, against the protruding foot of the bed. But in the old days . . . He turned to Roper.

'The door,' he said suddenly. 'The door.'

'What door?' Roper's voice was completely neutral.

'The door that's been taken down. It opened inwards—into the bedroom.' Clive pointed. 'You couldn't have seen them from here.'

'I don't know what you're talking about,' Roper said shortly. 'You can see for yourself: there's no door.'

'But there used to be. At the time of the—the murder. It was only recently the old people took it down. Mrs Preece mentioned it to me when I was here last autumn when Eddie was laid out dead in this room. They took the door down so that it would be easier for her to get to him if he should want anything in the night.'

'Very sensible. That door was a devil to open. The latch made such a clack.'

'And it screened much of the back room because it opened inwards. You couldn't have seen the foot of the bed.'

'Then I must have been further into the room.' Roper spoke easily, but his face had again gone white.

'It would make no difference,' Clive responded. 'You couldn't see them wherever you stood.'

'So?'

'So there's something wrong with your story. It can't have happened the way you describe.'

Roper's voice grew colder, more menacing. 'Are you trying to say that I lied?'

'Yes, I am. For your own good reasons.'

'What do you mean by that?'

'I mean—' Clive paused and swallowed—'that you have something ugly to hide.'

Roper laughed, and the sound was chilling. 'You've got a nerve, I must say. Are you by any chance accusing me of the murder?'

'Preece always maintained that it was you.'

'Preece was a bloody liar and a half-wit.'

'So I've heard. Invention wouldn't be such a man's strong point.'

'You forget—the jury decided he was lying.'

'Juries have made mistakes before now.'

'I don't know who you are,' Roper said with quiet fury, 'but by God I mean to find out. You'll retract that statement in public, unless you want to find yourself in court.'

'I may well find myself in court—as your accuser. It was you who murdered Elsie Preece.'

'Perhaps you'll be good enough to tell me how this crime was accomplished?'

'Quite easily. By manual pressure on the throat. You watched them all leave except Elsie, no doubt in the manner you describe. Then you stole in like a rat slinking into a corn-bin, and made your way up the stairs. Elsie was expecting you—she was half undressed already, but what happened then I can't guess. Perhaps there was a quarrel and you lost your temper; perhaps she told you she was giving you up. Perhaps, even, she was importunate and demanded money; or she may have tried blackmail—I don't know. Whatever the reason, you put an end to her, though, as you said of Preece, you may not have known what you did. But she was lying dead on the bed when you heard footsteps approaching. There was no escape, so you did the natural thing: you hid.'

'A very interesting reconstruction. Please go on with your detective story.'

'The intruder, of course, was Eddie Preece. Eddie had been suspicious of you for a long time—ever since his mother alerted him, in fact.'

'She always hated Elsie,' Roper muttered.

'This time Preece thought he'd catch you in the act. Instead, he found Elsie dead on the bed, half naked. He caught her to him, just as you describe, and for a moment they stood just as we saw them—or their shadows. Then he flung himself on the bed and cried.'

'I congratulate you on your imagination. But you can't prove any of this.'

'Perhaps not—though I'm not sure that I agree with you on that point. I'm certainly going to have a damn good try.'

'Try if you like, but not all your depositions will bring Eddie back from the grave.'

'Apart from justice, I owe it to myself to clear him.' Clive did not feel he could explain quite why. But with every word Roper spoke, he felt the sensation of guilt slip from him. Eddie's sins were whiter than snow. And therefore his sin-eater had a lesser load to carry. For the first time in a year Clive felt himself light of heart. He almost laughed aloud as he announced: 'I'm going to have this case re-opened. I shall go to London to see my lawyers for a start.'

'You won't, you know.' Roper spoke very softly. 'You're going to stay right here.'

There was so much menace in his tone that Clive was frightened, although he could see no reason for fear. Roper was stocky and well-muscled, but Clive was heavier. If he rushed Roper he could almost certainly get past him. He took a step forward.

Roper said harshly, 'That's enough.'

In spite of himself, Clive hesitated.

Roper said, 'It's as well for you you did. I'm not a karate-trained ex-commando for nothing. You move, and I'll break your neck.'

Clive felt the sweat of fear on his body. It was unbelievable that this should happen to him—to be alone in an empty house with an uncaught murderer who was preparing to murder again.

He made a gesture of protest.

'Are you going to keep still?' Roper asked.

'What are you going to do?' Clive demanded. He could scarcely speak for the chattering of his teeth.

'See you silenced for ever,' Roper replied brutally. 'You don't imagine you're going to walk out of here? I didn't ask you to come poking around in the first place. You've no one but yourself to blame.'

'You invited me in,' Clive said stupidly.

'Only because you'd seen the car in the lane. I couldn't afford to have it traced that I'd been here. From that moment it was inevitable you should die.'

Clive squared his shoulders. There could be no rescue; no one even knew where he was. He reproached himself for not having told the proprietor of the Red Lion of his destination, or even Barnabas Elms. But it would have made no difference to his present situation. He resolved to put up a fight, and was mentally rehearsing his tactics when something moving on the floor caught his eye. It was a shadow, but not his own shadow. He was standing still as any stone, whereas this shadow was inching forwards, its menacing hands upraised like giant claws. It was advancing with terrible deliberation on Roper, and whatever cast the shadow was emerging from the open bedroom door.

Clive dared not turn his head to look behind him. There was a coldness, a dankness chill as the grave. It grew in intensity as the caster of the shadow came closer, yet no footfall sounded on the floor. So grotesque and distorted was the shadow that it was impossible to tell if its original were equally so, or whether a normal even if not living being cast it. Clive found he was afraid to know.

Instead he gazed straight ahead at Roper, who had gone deathly pale at the sight of what approached. He seemed unable to move, unable to stop staring with eyeballs that bulged from his head. It was almost as though someone were choking him. His mouth opened but he made no sound; his pale face was suffused darkly; he tottered as if about to fall.

Clive was now enveloped in coldness. There was an earthy smell, as of something long underground. And the shadow now reached all the way to the far wall and began to ascend it, blotting out that corner of the room, blotting out the staircase, blotting out Roper, who gave a dreadful gurgling scream . . .

Clive was never certain if the darkness was because he fainted, although he heard the thunder of Roper's fall as he bumped and clattered down the staircase. The noise seemed as though it would never end. He put his hands to his ears to try to deaden it, but the sound reverberated in his head. By contrast, the silence that followed was absolute; it had the vaultlike quality of a tomb. Roper neither stirred nor spoke when Clive called him. It came home to him that Roper was dead.

The room seemed suddenly brighter and warmer, the overwhelming shadow had gone. Fearfully Clive looked behind him; the back bedroom was as empty as the front. There was nothing that could cast a shadow; the sky outside was cloudless October blue. Roper must have lost his balance and fallen; no other explanation would do.

Even so, the accident might be difficult to account for; there were no witnesses—not, at least, whom he could call. Clive went downstairs and touched Roper's warm, limp body. He was lying face downwards in a heap. With an effort, Clive turned him over, and gasped as his heart missed a beat. Roper's face was set in a mask of pure terror. There were the marks of manual strangulation on his throat.

Clive straightened up very slowly. In one way it was a logical end. So it was that Eddie Preece's sin-eater was arrested, charged with murder, and in due course tried and condemned.

Dearest Clarissa

Combe Tracy,
Tuesday, 19th April

Dearest Clarissa,

I'm sorry I didn't write to you last night, but I was too tired. Anyway, Jim will have told you we arrived safely. At least, I suppose he will; I asked him to ring you and he said he would when he got back to London. I feel terribly cut off down here.

Of course I know that's silly. I agreed to come here and I can leave again any time I want to, just as if it were an ordinary hotel. You've explained that very carefully and I quite understand. And I'm determined to be sensible and *not* leave—or not until they say I can. I've got to get better for Jim's sake. You've all explained that, too.

The journey down was perfectly easy. After we left the A 4 at Oxford, there wasn't much traffic about. Jim said the countryside was very beautiful, but I wasn't in the mood for noticing much. It was dark by the time we arrived here, so I only saw the sweep of gravel in front of the house, and a border of clipped yew hedges and glimpses of a high brick wall. I haven't been out of my room yet this morning, so I can't tell you very much more, except that the house was built about 1680—it says that on the portico of the front door.

They brought me my breakfast in bed this morning. I

must say they're terribly kind. And no one wears nurse's uniform or anything frightening; they wear flowered overalls instead. I wonder what they wear in the men's wing—sports coats and flannels, perhaps. And my window isn't barred—I was afraid it would be; it's just an ordinary sash.

Jim said my room looked very comfortable. I suppose in a way he's right. It's rather like a hotel room, except for the high hospital bed. And everything's so clean it glistens. I haven't seen Dr Braceman yet.

They say I'm to see him this morning. It's rather like waiting to see the Head. Do you remember how Miss Carlow always kept you waiting, after you'd knocked, for her little bell to ring? You could tell if you'd done anything awful because she kept you waiting such a long time; but if it was something pleasant, you went in straight away. I don't suppose you ever had to wait, Clarissa; you never did awful things like me. I mean, you weren't careless and forgetful and bottom of the form and hopeless at games, and plain on top of it all. No one could ever understand how I came to be your sister. It was like a let-down all round, what with Daddy being so disappointed that I wasn't the son he'd hoped for, and then me not even being a satisfactory sort of girl. I still can't get over Jim marrying me, especially when he could have had you, but it was easily the best thing that ever happened to me. If only I hadn't let him down too!

My room is long and rather narrow. It's evidently been made by partitioning a bigger room in half. The partition must be pretty thick, though; I can't hear a sound from next door. Perhaps there isn't anyone next door. It's so odd, not knowing. And if there is, she must be mad, like me.

Because that's what you all mean, although nobody says it. A 'nervous breakdown' is a polite phrase for being temporarily insane. Not that I feel insane; I just can't pull myself together. I keep crying over silly things. But you all think I'm mad, though none of you dares say so. That's why you've sent me here—'Combe Tracy for rest and mental recuperation', or whatever it was it said in the brochure. But you needn't think I don't know what I'm doing—or what you're doing, come to that.

I've been sent here because I'm in the way, I've become a nuisance. I don't think Jim can bear the sight of me. Not that I blame him. A wife who can't even manage to become a mother is a bit much for any man to take. If only I'd been more careful coming downstairs when you called me—and that's a dreadful thing to say because it sounds as if I'm blaming you, whereas if you hadn't been there to get the doctor, I suppose I might easily have died. How I wish I had! It would have been the best thing that could have happened. And after a decent interval, you could have married Jim. There! Now you know my last wish if anything should happen. I tried to say this to Jim, but he wouldn't listen. Sometimes it's easier to write things down.

I've always loved writing letters. There are things I can write that I could never, ever say—even to you, because you're so much cleverer than I am that I'm always afraid of looking or sounding a fool. But when I write, I don't have to watch other people's reactions. I don't have to see them getting bored, or smiling in the wrong places, or preparing to demolish my arguments. I don't start to say something and wish I'd never begun.

I wonder what the other 'inmates' will be like? Meeting them is one of the things I dread. I was so afraid of going down to breakfast that I lay awake half the night. Then, when they brought my breakfast to my room, I was so relieved I just turned all the taps on. You can't imagine what an idiot I felt. I thought of the flowery-overalled woman going back to tell Dr Braceman, and how he'd think I was really off my head. I cried so much I couldn't eat my breakfast, and the coffee had all gone cold. And when the flowery-overalled woman came for the tray, she said nothing. I felt about six years old.

I didn't finish this morning because they came to say Dr Braceman would see me and would I go to his room. His room's on the ground floor, so I went downstairs—there's a beautiful staircase—and knocked on Dr Braceman's door. The door says 'Medical Superintendent' and there's a smell of disinfectant mixed with the flowers, but otherwise you'd never know you were in a hospital; it's just like a big country house. Dr Braceman doesn't even look like a doctor; he wears tweeds and smokes a pipe and looks like a country squire. And he said 'Come in' at once, so I knew it wasn't going to be too awful. In fact, I quite enjoyed myself.

No, Clarissa, I am *not* falling in love with Dr Braceman, although I can quite understand how someone could. He seems to be so interested in what you're saying and he doesn't ask questions or make you feel you're ill. Indeed, almost the only questions he asked were about you—I hope you're flattered. He wanted to know where you lived and what you did, and whether we looked alike and what was the age-gap between us, and whether we'd been to the same school. I gave you a pretty good build-up, everything from your being head girl on. He said he'd like to meet you, Clarissa, and I was to introduce you if ever you came down! Then he said he usually had a cup of coffee about eleven, and he hoped I'd have one too. So I said yes please and told him how I'd missed out on breakfast. Evidently flowery-overall hadn't let on! He said he often didn't bother with breakfast, and asked me what I thought of the house. I said I hadn't seen it yet, but I was surprised it was as early as 1680, the main staircase seemed much later than that.

Dr Braceman said it was—nearly a hundred years later, and added that most people wouldn't have noticed that. I told him I was interested in old buildings and history, and he said in that case I'd come to the right spot.

For three hundred years this house belonged to the Bellenger family. Before that there was a priory here, but the Bellengers acquired the land after the Dissolution, pulled down the buildings and erected a fortified manor house instead. They fought for the King in the Civil War and the house was burnt down as a reprisal by Colonel Skinner and his Parliamentary troops. After the Restoration, Charles II raised Bellenger to the peerage and gave him some mono-polies. The new house was begun with the proceeds in 1680, and finished twelve years later by his son; but it was under the third earl, or rather his countess, that the whole inside was re-done.

Dr Braceman said I could read all about it in the library, and if I'd finished my coffee he'd show me some of the books straight away. And do you know, I had finished it, without noticing, and a plate of biscuits as well!

I shan't have time to finish this letter before the post goes, and there's so much else I want to say. I'll write again tomorrow. Keep safe, darling, and keep an eye on my dear Jim for me.

Your loving sister,
Julia

Combe Tracy,
Wednesday, 20th April

Dearest Clarissa,

This is a very odd place because it isn't odd at all, if
you understand me. You just expect it to be. I got lost last
night after dinner, trying to get from the dining-room to the
library, and a very nice woman asked if she could help me—
I took her for one of the staff. She was about fifty, tall and
rather full-bosomed, with a deep, commanding voice—
musical, but you wouldn't dream of not doing what she told
you. She knew who I was, too. My dear, I found out later
she's one of the patients; she's been here eighteen months. I
wonder what's wrong? She seemed to have such presence.
I'd give anything to be as poised as that.

I've now met several of the patients, men and women. We
have meals together and sit together in the lounge. We're
not encouraged to talk about our illnesses, but if we want to,
no one really minds. Some talk and some don't, that's about
it. On the whole I prefer the ones who don't. One thing: no
one ever asks you what's the matter. You can say as much or
as little as you like.

The girl in the room next to me is named Tessa Newton. I
feel awful to think I wrote that she was mad. She's the
sanest, gentlest person you could imagine—I can't think why
she has to be 'inside'. She's very small and dainty, beautifully dressed, with the most enormous, haunting eyes. She
loves clothes—she's some sort of fashion artist—and a most
amusing mimic, too. I told her about the lady with the
commanding presence. She knew at once who I meant. And
Clarissa, would you believe it! It seems the commanding
presence took to going about without her clothes. That's

why they had to send her to Combe Tracy. She still does it from time to time. Yet she doesn't look as if she knows the meaning of the word 'naked'. I'll never get used to this place.

Perhaps I shan't need to get used to it, because Dr Braceman said this morning that he hoped mine wouldn't have to be a long stay. He said I was a very lucky woman if I would but realize it, and he hoped natural intelligence would come to my aid. According to him, the trouble with most of his patients is that they aren't loved enough, or not in the right way, whereas he couldn't see that I had much to complain of on that score. I felt so ungrateful I started to cry. I decided to ring Jim up to tell him I was sorry (though I didn't tell Dr Braceman that). We can make 'phone calls here from a booth in the hall, so last night I rang Jim but there wasn't any answer. It was about nine o'clock, and he's always home by half past seven, but last night he wasn't home at half past ten, which is when we have to be in bed. I tried three times, and the 'phone kept ringing and ringing. I told myself he must be out. But it's so unlike him, Clarissa; I don't understand it. I can't wait to ring again tonight.

I shan't ring the office because he made me promise I wouldn't, unless it was a matter of life and death. I must keep *some* control, even if I am unbalanced. After all, the commanding presence doesn't go naked all the time!

Isn't it funny, heaps of women lose a baby (Dr Braceman pointed this out), but they don't all allow their grief to prey on them, as I have. You can never tell how people will react. I tried to tell him that it wasn't only losing the baby; it's the feeling that it's all my fault. If I hadn't run downstairs I shouldn't have tripped and fallen. Because you know, Clarissa, I *did* trip. I didn't stumble or miss my footing. I fell over some obstacle. Except that there is no obstacle on our staircase. And yet I'm not imagining things. In the split second before I started falling, when I tried to clutch the banister rail, I remember thinking 'Whatever is it?' And then I don't remember anything more, except you telling me to lie still and the doctor coming and the fear inside me that was greater than the pain. But if I hadn't been in such a hurry I should have seen the obstacle. That's what I can't explain.

I must write to Jim. I'll write again before the week's out. I wish so much that you were here. It feels like the first time I had to go back to school without you. I can't explain why. Never mind.

Love from
Julia

Combe Tracy,
Friday, 22nd April

Dearest Clarissa,

Thank you for your letter. I never thought that Jim might be with you. It's so good of you to invite him. I'm sure you're right to say it's bad for him to be alone. It wouldn't do for Jim to brood himself silly also, would it? I'll try to be more sensible next time.

As for your saying I mustn't be deceived by an appearance of normality, there isn't much danger of that. We had the most horrible scene last night at dinner. I can't get it out of my mind. We sit at tables for four and we can choose our places, only woe betide you if you take an old resident's place! I sit with Tessa, and we were joined last night by a youngish bald man named Lovegrove, and by a Major

Armstrong, an upright elderly man. I didn't say much—
Tessa does most of the talking—and we got through the soup
all right. Then, when the main course came—it was steak-
and-kidney pudding—Major Armstrong looked round at us
and said: 'I should advise you all not to touch this. I happen
to know that it's been poisoned.' Tessa said 'Nonsense' and
took a mouthful to prove it. Lovegrove also picked up his
knife and fork. Major Armstrong became very excited and
tried to grab hold of his arm. He said the food contained
sodium chloride, and Lovegrove laughed and said that was
only common salt, and he ought to know because he was a
chemist! Armstrong stood up and began to shout.

He used the filthiest language, and raved on and on about
a plot to poison him. He was crying, and said it was only to
be expected because he had poisoned his wife. Two attend-
ants from the male wing came to stop him—they do wear
sports coats, Clarissa, fancy that!—but he threw his plate on
the floor and became quite violent. In the end they had to
drag him out.

I couldn't finish my dinner. In any case it had gone cold
by then. It wasn't that I thought it was poisoned, but I
couldn't forget what he'd said about his wife. Do we really
have murderers among us? And how on earth can you tell?
I don't expect you to answer that question, but you will
understand how I feel.

I'm glad you realize that I didn't really mean it when I
accused you of trying to put me away. I was upset. Nuff
sed?

Jim is coming down at the week-end. I can't wait to show
him this place.

Your loving sister,
Julia

Combe Tracy,
Tuesday, 26th April

Dearest Clarissa,

It was wonderful to see Jim on Sunday, and wonderful to see you too. How good of you to bother to come such a long way. Of course it was company for Jim.

I so enjoyed showing you the gardens. I think they're beautiful, except for the formal garden, which I find frightening. Those tall yew-hedges are so solid and dark. They've been there since the eighteenth century. Just think of all the things they must have seen! I feel there must be ghosts among those yew-hedges; it would be fitting. After all, the yew is a churchyard tree. And the fact that the flower-beds and paths have given way to greensward makes it more than ever like a burial-ground.

I'm sorry you didn't think I was looking better. Jim did; at least, he said he did. But that's the trouble; I no longer trust what people tell me. Major Armstrong, for instance, didn't poison his wife. He just thinks he did because there was once a man called Armstrong who did, and nearly got away with it. Dr Braceman told me so when I asked him if there were really murderers among us. He said Major Armstrong wouldn't hurt a fly. He also said there were plenty of murderers among us, but unfortunately they couldn't be caught because they didn't use a knife or a bullet or poison; they simply drove other people to death, sometimes by self-destruction, sometimes by robbing them of the will to live. He also said I was a natural victim!!! Can you imagine such a thing? I told him jokingly that I should be very suspicious in future, and he said quite seriously that that was good.

Do you know what Dr Braceman has suggested? He wants me to write a history of this house. He says the material's all there in the library; it just hasn't been put together till now. He says a lot of people would be interested in it; he would himself for one. Tomorrow I shall take a look at what's available. It might be rather fun.

I asked Dr Braceman if there were any ghosts here, and he said very firmly that he didn't believe in ghosts. Which is rather the answer I expected, though I'm not at all sure that I agree. Do you think there are ghosts, Clarissa? I don't remember ever asking you before. Tessa says she's sure there are ghosts, she's seen them, but Tessa likes to pose as being fey. You know, Tessa does pose. She's not a fashion artist; it's just that that's what she thinks she'd like to be. It's rather like Major Armstrong, isn't it, only silly instead of sad. Poor Tessa, she's a secretary really; perhaps I was wrong and she *is* a little mad.

Major Armstrong is back in circulation. Since the poison business he's kept to his room. He seems perfectly normal; in fact, he's rather pleasant. And he's not a scrap embarrassed. I'd die. Dr Braceman says he probably doesn't realize what happened. How confusing everything is down here. Dr Braceman says it's a good sign I think so. He says he thinks I'll soon be home again.

Ever your loving sister,
Julia

Combe Tracy,
Wednesday, 4th May

Dearest Clarissa,

I was delighted to get another letter from you, until I opened it and found it contained the news it did. Of course that's terribly selfish of me. I ought to be thrilled for Jim's sake that the firm wants to send him to New York, only I can't think of anything except how much I want him near me, and New York's three thousand miles away. I wish I were well enough to go with him, but I'm afraid there's not much chance of that.

As a matter of fact they kept me in bed yesterday and wouldn't let me write letters. I think they gave me drugs. Anyway, I couldn't think clearly about anything, not even about Jim going to New York. When I first read your letter after breakfast, I kept telling myself that a month wasn't very long. But each time I thought about it, it got longer. I felt as if I would never see Jim again.

When I went in to see Dr Braceman, he knew at once I was upset. He asked me—very kindly—what was the matter, and I'm afraid I just broke down and cried. I must have been quite hysterical, because I didn't even know what I said, but he got the gist of it all right, and said rather coldly that he was surprised Jim hadn't told him. And then I did an awful thing.

I didn't mean to do it, Clarissa. It was simply that I had no idea how he'd react; but I'm afraid I've got you in bad with Dr Braceman because I said you'd told me about it in a letter, and he seemed quite cross that you had. I told him that you had only done it to save me, because you knew how I would feel if Jim came down next week-end and sprang it on me, and he said that wasn't for you to judge. I got rather overwrought, and accused him of being unpleasant because he didn't like you, though I don't know what made me say that, except that you said you didn't like *him*, and these things are always mutual. Do you remember how you and Aunt Sophie fought?

She's the only other person I can think of who hasn't liked you, and she was a horrid old bitch, although I shouldn't say that because she's dead now, and she left me all that money. I'd no idea she was so rich. But even in death she tried to sow dissension; she didn't leave anything to you; and that could easily have led to quarrels if you weren't so generous-hearted that her nasty little scheme fell through. Anyway, I've left half of it to you if there are no more children; Jim gets the other half.

What made me think of Aunt Sophie was Dr Braceman and the way I made things worse the more I explained. He was determined to misunderstand me, and in this he succeeded pretty well. I won't tell you what he said, but he twisted everything. Aunt Sophie used to do the same. The more I defended you, the more she was annoyed by it. She would have loved to see us fight. And you too, my poor Clarissa, were affected by it; you couldn't do anything right. Even the snapshots of you she took at my wedding came out badly, although she tried to pretend it was only the light.

All the other pictures of you as my bridesmaid were beautiful. I was quite outshone, except that people make such a fuss of a bride—as I hope you'll discover some day, darling, though why a girl as lovely as you hasn't married is something I'll never know. But Aunt Sophie took the most cruel pictures. You really looked eaten up with hate, although it was only because you were off guard and not smiling; you didn't even know you were being snapped. I told Aunt Sophie she'd taken an unfair advantage, but she only sniffed—you remember that trick she had. After she was dead and I was going through her papers I found the prints and the negative and burnt them. So they don't exist any more.

It all goes to show that if you think people are evil, they'll *be* evil. I tried to tell Dr Braceman that, but he said he wasn't convinced of the subjectivity of evil. That's an odd saying from a man who doesn't believe in ghosts!

I'm afraid the history of Combe Tracy isn't progressing very rapidly. These last two days have set it back a bit. And now I can't think of anything but that Jim will be coming on Saturday. I wonder what he'll have to say.

Clarissa, I want you to know that you did right to tell me —I mean about Jim going to New York. If Dr Braceman says you shouldn't have done, you can tell him I said so. You've always known me better than anyone else.

I'm tired tonight, so I think I'll stop writing—or scribbling, as Tessa would say. Did I tell you Tessa was frightfully superstitious? I only discovered that today. We were walking in the grounds—not the formal garden; Tessa hates that as much as I do—when a black cat crossed our path. I said it meant good luck, but it seems it crossed from left to right, which is terribly unlucky. Poor Tessa looked really scared. Then she saw a magpie—one for sorrow—and she got so worked up we had to go indoors, where the first thing she saw was a pair of shoes on the hall table. She said it meant a death in the house. I said it meant that someone had left a pair of shoes there for a moment, but she would have none of it. She stayed in her room and refused to come down at lunch-time. But she seems to have got over it tonight.

Your loving sister,
Julia

Combe Tracy,
Wednesday, 11th May

Dearest Clarissa,

Jim came down on Saturday as promised, but Dr Braceman saw him first, so Jim knew all that had happened as a result of your letter before I had a chance to tell him myself.

Clarissa, imagine the situation! Jim said he wasn't going just as I'd steeled myself to be brave and let him go. He said he'd turned it down and hadn't been going to tell me anything about it. So I should have failed him again and I shouldn't even have known. Because it would have been a step up in his career—I forced that admission out of him—but for my sake it was something he would forgo. He said it meant more to him to have me back to normal. As if my normal self were good enough for him!

I begged him to go, but he said Dr Braceman had advised against it. Whereupon I went to Dr Braceman at once. He had visitors, and it was dreadfully awkward, but I didn't care any more what I said. I told him that if Jim turned down a chance like that for my sake, I should never forgive myself. I said it was bad enough now, being so unworthy, but if I had to live with that I'd kill myself. Jim of course kept trying to stop me, and the visitors were sitting goggle-eyed. Dr Braceman said he'd come and talk to us later, and with that Jim got me outside.

He said if I was going to get worked up now because he *wasn't* going, he was damned if he knew what to do. He went back later and talked it over with Dr Braceman and in the end they decided he should go, because I might reproach myself more if he didn't than I'd upset myself while he was away.

Needless to say, I've been in bed since all this happened, but I feel calmer again today. And, dearest Clarissa, it's thanks to you there's a happy ending. If I didn't have you, I don't know what I'd do.

Ever your loving sister,
Julia

Combe Tracy,
Saturday, 14th May

Dearest Clarissa,

Jim leaves today, in an hour's time. He rang me up last night to say goodbye. I tried to sound cheerful for his sake, but I feel as if I'm going to die. I don't mean I feel ill; it's just a horrid conviction that I'm never going to see Jim again. Or perhaps it's Jim who's going to die—that would amount to the same thing, wouldn't it? Suppose something happens to his plane!

I will not think about that. Let's talk of something different. Clarissa, do you know, this place really does have a ghost. I found an account of it in an old book yesterday. It's a girl who was drowned near here.

Have I told you about the lake? It's beyond the formal

garden. There are two lakes, but one's silted up. It's full of mud and sedge, and there's very little water. But the other looks deep enough. They're fed from the river, which is out of sight beyond the brick wall, and the lakes themselves are supposed to be out of bounds. But you can get to them quite easily if you want to, only there isn't a lot of point. There's a family of moorhens on the lake proper, which Dr Braceman says is about five feet deep. It's part of the priory fishponds, which became the moat surrounding the manor, the one that Colonel Skinner burnt down in 1645.

The ghost is the ghost of Dorothea Bellenger, the eldest daughter of the house. She was betrothed to a young man of a neighbouring family at the time of the Civil War. Then his family sided with the Parliament, while hers of course was for the King. The betrothal was called off and Dorothea was broken-hearted, but her beloved found a way to keep in touch. With the help of a servant, they used to smuggle letters and were soon planning to elope. Dorothea, disguised as a washerwoman, was to slip through the guard at the gates and meet her lover at the cross-roads leading to the village; from there they would cross the fields to the river bank. There was an old ford, little used since the bridge had been built a hundred years earlier, and they planned to wade across. On the other side her lover had horses waiting, and an escort of mounted men.

All went well until they reached the river, which was shrouded in thick white mist. We've had several of these river-mists lately, and you can't see your hand before your face. Anyway, they mistook the crossing, or perhaps Dorothea's foot slipped. She was swept downstream, and when her lover tried to seize her, the current carried him away as well.

I think it's a beautiful, sad story, and so does Tessa. I told her about it last night. But she says she hopes none of us ever sees Dorothea, because ghosts only appear to those who are about to die. I told her she mustn't believe that, but the legend says much the same. Apparently a girl in a long white dress glides among the yew-hedges of the formal garden, and beckons to those she has come to fetch. There are several recorded instances of her appearance, and each time it's been followed by a death. Mr Lovegrove, to whom we were talking at dinner, was sceptical about the whole thing; scientists always are. I shan't tell Dr Braceman about Dorothea. I somehow don't think he'd approve. He'd think I was getting morbid fancies, like the way I feel about Jim. Oh Clarissa, he's in the air now, and every second he's going farther away. If only I could have gone too, or he could have waited! I feel so terribly alone. But it's only for four weeks, and I'll get used to it. I couldn't have stood in Jim's way.

Take no notice of your silly, but loving

Julia

Combe Tracy,
Friday, 20th May

Dearest Clarissa,

You are a wonderful sister! How good of you to say you'll come down. You have no idea how the thought of seeing you lifts my spirits. Bless you. Roll on Sunday!

Love,

Julia

Combe Tracy,
Sunday, 22nd May

Dearest Clarissa,

Something so horrible has happened that although it's only a few hours since you left me, I feel I must write to you at once. Clarissa, I've seen Dorothea Bellenger's ghost.

It was after dinner on Sunday, and I was sitting in my room looking out at the garden, just as I told you I always do. In the past, I've regretted that my window overlooked the formal garden, but now I don't mind it a bit since you pointed out to me when you were here that I can see the road and that you could stop the car and wave to me as you were passing—just as in fact you did.

Well, I was sitting there after dinner, and I must admit I was a bit upset. I mean, I hadn't expected Jim would do that—with my own sister, least of all. Of course I understand now more than ever why you wanted him safely in New York, and of course I know, dearest Clarissa, that because you're you nothing wrong actually took place All the same, I hadn't supposed that Jim of all men would make a pass at you, although when you come to think of it, the poor darling has been starved lately and he can't be blamed for thinking you're beautiful. So really I'm not reproaching anyone—I'm just terribly, terribly sad. And I must admit also I'm a bit frightened. I expect there are gorgeous girls in New York.

But I hadn't been crying or anything silly. In fact, I was rather pleased with myself. When I thought that a few weeks ago I'd wept at the idea of going down to breakfast, I realized how much better I was.

And then, while I was sitting at the window, I saw

Dorothea Bellenger's ghost. I saw her quite clearly in the twilight, moving in and out of those dark clumps of yew. She looked down as she walked and twisted her hands before her, a little like Lady Macbeth. She had long hair that fell forward over her shoulder—grey hair, yet you could tell she was young. She was wearing a stiff white dress that didn't flow with her body, and her movements were very odd. She didn't walk—she glided among the hedges, as if she took long steps and her feet never touched the ground.

I couldn't believe it for a moment—I thought the light was playing tricks. But when she came back it was no longer possible to pretend she didn't exist. I wanted to go for help or call somebody—but suppose they didn't see her too? Suppose they said I was worse, that I had hallucinations, that I was really and truly mad? Then they'd shut me away behind bars for ever, and I should never see Jim or you again. Clarissa, do *you* think I'm mad? If I am, I can't bear it. I'd a thousand times rather be dead.

Perhaps I shall be dead, because just then Dorothea turned and looked full at me, as if she knew I'd be there. She raised her hand and—very slowly—beckoned. Then she stepped back and beckoned once again. By now she was almost hidden by the yew hedge. She raised her hand as if to beckon again and disappeared. Suddenly she wasn't there any longer. I was trembling. I've never been so scared.

I can't tell Dr Braceman or Tessa or any of the others. Clarissa, what do *you* think? Write soon, write at once, I can bear anything except not knowing.

Your loving sister,
Julia

Combe Tracy,
Friday, 27th May

Dearest Clarissa,

I wrote on Sunday that I could bear anything except not knowing, but when your letter arrived today—almost a week later—I felt I was well served for saying anything so rash.

Clarissa, you don't mean it, do you? You don't really think I'm mad? You say 'as you yourself recognized at the outset', and I believe I did write something like that. But it was only because I was upset at having to come here. Don't you think you'd have felt the same? I tell you, Clarissa, I'm *not* mad—I swear it—but how can I convince you I'm sane?

As for my 'previous hallucinations' that you refer to, I don't know what you mean. Do you mean my saying I tripped over something on the staircase? That wasn't a hallucination, that was true. I ought to know; I was the one who fell and lost Jim's baby. You were only standing by. Oh, I know you saved my life but you couldn't do otherwise, could you? You couldn't very well have let me die.

You say: 'As you have already noticed, all the inmates of Combe Tracy have their little peculiarities.' I suppose you think seeing ghosts is my particular quirk? It's true no one else has seen the ghost of Dorothea Bellenger, but would you believe in her existence if they had? You're not obliged to accept anything that anyone here tells you. You've got the perfect excuse: we're all mad.

You remind me of Major Armstrong's 'hallucination' about believing he poisoned his wife. But Clarissa, that's not at all the same thing as seeing a beckoning figure among the yew-hedges. And there was *no* river-mist about that night.

I've had a letter from Jim—a long one. He says he's having a marvellous time. I keep wondering if the words have any significance, but I can't really believe they have. You say I must remember that Jim is 'very normal'. I'm not in danger of forgetting that. It's why I worry that I'm no good to him. I couldn't blame him if he did find someone else.

Suppose I see Dorothea again and she beckons? She seems to be beckoning me towards the lake. Is she suggesting what I ought to do to make Jim happy? If only there was someone I could tell!

But I'm sure you're right about not telling Dr Braceman. He'd think I'd had a serious relapse. Whereas perhaps if I keep it to myself I can fight it. It may never happen again. If a week goes by and I don't see her, I shall know my imagination was playing tricks. But if I do . . . Oh Clarissa, I *know* something dreadful's going to happen. Pray that I'm wrong about this.

Ever your loving sister,
Julia

Combe Tracy,
Monday, 30th May

Dearest Clarissa,

Tessa has seen Dorothea! Do you think now you could believe? Because I hadn't told Tessa or anyone about it, so she's an independent witness, isn't she?

Once again, it was just after dinner, the time when I'm

usually in my room. But last night I'd gone to the library to fetch some books I wanted. As I was coming back, Tessa's door flew open, and she ran out, looking like death. She was trembling and shivering and crying; I was a rock by comparison. She's so superstitious, that's the trouble. She's convinced it means she's going to die. I told her not to be ridiculous, because it must have been meant for me. It was only by chance that she'd seen it. But she would have none of it.

I begged her to tell Dr Braceman, but she said he'd think she'd been making it up—like that business about her being a fashion-artist. I told you, she has these fantasies. I offered to tell him that I'd seen the ghost last Sunday, but she said that wouldn't do any good. We'd both be suspect and be made to stay here longer, which of course is exactly what you said.

Tessa was making such a commotion, I was afraid one of the staff would hear, and I couldn't think what explanation we could offer. Eventually I got Tessa back into her room. She had calmed down a little, but she still seemed very frightened. She didn't want me to leave her alone. She said Dorothea distinctly raised her hand and beckoned. She did this three times and disappeared.

All the time I was trying to comfort Tessa, I was really comforting myself. Because I'm quite certain I was the one Dorothea came to summon, only Tessa happened to see her instead. She came last Sunday and she's come again this one —same place, same hour, same day. But we're the only ones to see her because our windows overlook the formal garden, whereas everyone else's look out to front or back.

Clarissa, if I die, if Dorothea comes to fetch me, remember what I said about Jim. He's very fond of you—I've always known that—even before he made a pass at you. I'd like you to have him, if I can't. You'll be a better wife than I've been, and mother too. And the money Aunt Sophie left would be very useful. I told you, it's divided between you two.

It would be better if I died. I'm no good to anyone, and I've never been the right wife for Jim. I can't even pull myself together enough to take action. If I had done, poor Tessa needn't have been scared.

Jim writes often. He continues to have a good time. He is very solicitous, but I am not deceived. Life would be more fun for him if his wife weren't a mentally sick woman. When I die, I don't think he'll even feel grieved.

Don't bother to come down this Sunday. I'm afraid I'm too much on edge. This sense of something horrible hanging over me is beginning to get me down. But if Dorothea doesn't appear this Sunday I'll feel better, so come down the following week.

Tessa hasn't left her room today. I feel dreadful. It's all my fault and yet I dare not speak.

Your loving but distraught
Julia

Combe Tracy,
Wednesday, 1st June

Dearest Clarissa,

I couldn't write to you yesterday. It was the most dreadful day I've ever known, except for the day I lost the baby. Tessa committed suicide.

I can't believe it's really happened. She was found hanging in her room. She used the cord of her dressing-gown. One of the nurses found her. I didn't know about it till afterwards.

She didn't come down to breakfast, but I didn't think anything of that because I thought she was still upset about seeing Dorothea. Then Dr Braceman sent for me. He told me Tessa was dead.

He thought I might have heard something in the night, and of course I had heard comings and goings and voices on the landing outside. Once I even fancied I heard his voice, but decided I must be mistaken. But as usual I was stupid and misunderstood him. He meant he thought I might have heard when Tessa died. It seems she strangled quite slowly, but mercifully our walls are thick. Isn't it terrible that someone as young and pretty as Tessa should choose to destroy herself like that? It seems she'd tried it before—Dr Braceman told me—but they'd thought she was getting on so well. Dr Braceman looked grey. I was sorry for him. He said he'd never had a failure like that.

Clarissa, I may be a fool, but I told him about Dorothea, and how Tessa believed it was a sign she was going to die. He didn't say anything, but he listened until I'd finished and then he asked me why I hadn't come to him. I didn't know what to say, I felt so wicked; I could feel him blaming me for Tessa's death, although of course he said he wasn't when I asked him. He said Tessa was suicidally inclined. He said her death was his fault if it was anyone's, for thinking her more recovered than she was. He said I'd had a good effect upon her—but I couldn't bear any more.

I started to cry hysterically, like I used to do when I first came here. He was very kind. He asked me if I thought I was going to die because of 'this ridiculous spectre', and I said I only wished I could. He asked me a lot about Dorothea—

what time she appeared, and where, and could I show him how she walked, and stood, and beckoned, and what kind of clothes did she wear. He wanted to know if I could see through her. I told him I didn't think I'd tried. Whereupon he said he'd a good mind to try next Sunday, as a scientific experiment. I told him he was welcome to sit in my room, but he said he thought he'd keep out of sight. Dorothea might be frightened if she saw another person, but if she saw only me, it would be all right.

I don't mind having Dr Braceman for company, but suppose he doesn't see her and I do? He'll know then that I'm much worse than when I came here. Do you think I'm incurable?

Clarissa, when you come next Sunday, couldn't you see him? I know you don't like him, but for my sake—please! If you could just confirm what I've said in my letters. He might take more notice of you. That's the trouble with being 'mental'—no one believes you, except poor Tessa, and look at her! I still can't believe it's happened. Did I tell you she was an only child?

Oh God, isn't it awful for her parents? And to think it ought to have been me. That's why I'm sure Dorothea will come again to fetch me. If she does, darling, remember all I've said.

Your loving sister,
Julia

Combe Tracy,
Monday, 6th June

Dearest Clarissa,

Thank you for coming yesterday. I am sorry I got so upset. It was what you said about poor Tessa that did it. I felt guilty enough without that. Do you really think I'm responsible for what happened, because I told Tessa about Dorothea's ghost? It's true I knew Tessa was superstitious, but I never thought the ghost might appear. I didn't believe in ghosts, Clarissa—at least not until I saw this. Even now I don't know if it's something real or something imagined, like the witches and the dagger in *Macbeth*. I asked Dr Braceman if he thought I was mad, and he said soothingly of course I wasn't, but I don't feel I'll ever be sure.

I'm sorry you wouldn't see Dr Braceman, though perhaps you're right and relatives shouldn't interfere. And of course Jim will be home in a fortnight. That's a wonderfully comforting thought.

At least it would be if I weren't so frightened. He seems to be having such a good time. He writes me long and loving letters, but suppose he's just doing that to be kind? Jim *is* kind; no one knows that better than I do; and perhaps for that reason he lies. I keep thinking about what you say he said in your letter, about making the most of his time. I feel I ought to give him his freedom, yet if I asked him if he wanted it, he'd say no. Is that why Dorothea comes and beckons—to show me the way I should go?

But she didn't come last night, Clarissa. I promised to let you know. Dr Braceman came upstairs with me after dinner, and he sat at the back of the room, where he couldn't be seen from the window. I took my usual place. It was a lovely evening, very mild and pleasant, with a pale green sky and a young moon. I could see every detail of the formal garden, even to the gathering dew. But there wasn't a sign of Dorothea. I looked until my eyes stood out on stalks. When it was fairly obvious she wasn't coming, Dr Braceman came to the window too. I was afraid he'd think I'd invented the whole thing, even the part about Tessa, but he didn't seem as if he did. He asked me which direction Dorothea came from, where she stood, and where she disappeared. I couldn't remember exactly, but I said it was near where you stood and waved. Then I realized I hadn't told him about that bit, so I had to explain that as well. I think he was bored—he quickly got back to 'the apparition', as he called it, but I'd told him all there was to tell.

He said I should stop worrying about Dorothea. That's when I asked him if he thought I was mad. I suggested he should come and watch with me next Sunday, but he said he couldn't because he'd be away. I must have looked horrified, because he laughed aloud at my expression and said even a medical superintendent had to have some private life. I felt awful, because apparently he goes away every six weeks, only I hadn't been here long enough to find out.

I said I should spend next Sunday evening in the library, and he gave me a funny sort of look and asked if I was really so frightened of 'the apparition'. I didn't know what to say. If you're afraid of something, people say you should go out and face it, but I don't think I could bear to do such a thing. So I didn't say anything. He seemed quite satisfied and let it go at that.

As we went back through the hall a funny thing happened. The 'commanding presence' came sailing out of her

room. She pirouetted and turned in front of us like a manne-
quin, and Clarissa, she hadn't a stitch on! I didn't know
where to look, I was so embarrassed, but Dr Braceman
didn't seem to mind. He asked her if she didn't feel cold with
no clothes on, and hadn't she better go back to her room.
Her eyes narrowed—they're brown eyes, rather cunning,
with heavy pouches underneath—and she came right up
close to me—I could smell her—and said in a sort of hiss:
'You do it with your clothes on, don't you? Don't think I
don't know what you do, when you have the doctor in your
room for hours together. You're not a patient, you're his
private whore!'

Dr Braceman said: 'That's enough, Mrs Curtis'—very
coldly. 'Kindly go back to you room.' She pirouetted and
said archly, 'Shall I see you in a moment, Doctor? Or haven't
you the stamina?' But she went, that was what surprised
me. Dr Braceman pulled out his keys, selected one and locked
the door behind her. At once she started to scream. I've
never heard such obscenities. She was so angry she even got
the words muddled up. I just stood there, I couldn't even
make myself move forward. Dr Braceman led me away. As
we recrossed the hall he said gently: 'And you ask me if *you*
are mad!' I felt a lot better after that, though it's awful to
say so. At least I'm not that bad!

Clarissa, what did you mean when you were here on
Sunday about 'the valuable presence of the lake'? It was
when you asked me where it was and I reminded you that it
was out of bounds for patients, and you said something
about that being a mistake. I remember saying I thought
it very sensible, and you said we weren't going to quarrel about that. But the remark's been puzzling me ever

since you made it. Surely *you* don't think I ought to drown myself?

I'm tired tonight. It's weeks since I did anything at the History but I must. I promised Dr Braceman I would.

Take care of yourself, dearest Clarissa. I feel so lonely always, after you've gone.

Your loving sister,
Julia

Combe Tracy,
Friday, 10th June

Dearest Clarissa,

I oughtn't to have asked you in my last letter if you wanted me to drown myself. Of course I was only joking, and as I told you, I was extremely tired. I can quite understand why you are angry, but please don't be. You are the only relative I've got, with Jim on the other side of the Atlantic. Even Dr Braceman's going away.

Do please come on Sunday. Otherwise I shall have to spend the day alone. I shan't even have Tessa for company. The funeral was yesterday. They had to wait until the inquest was over. Dr Braceman went to both, in a black tie. I've never seen a man look so much older. And so sad it makes me want to cry.

Please accept this apology, Clarissa. I didn't in the least mean what you think. You say I write like a madwoman and you're heartily sorry for Jim, but couldn't you be a bit sorry for me and come on Sunday? I shan't need to ask you again, because the next week Jim will be home and I'll be his 'liability', as you put it. Do please, please come on Sunday. My love as always till then.

Ever your loving sister,
Julia

Combe Tracy,
Sunday, 12th June

Dearest Clarissa,

This is the last letter I shall ever write to you. I am going to drown myself. In the lake, whose presence will indeed be valuable. As always, you were absolutely right.

I don't think I need give explanations. You know what a failure I am. I can't even keep friends with my own sister, because if I could you would have come today. I kidded myself all week that because you hadn't written, it didn't mean you weren't coming, but when it got to half past four I knew you weren't. I should like to have seen you, but since that isn't to be, I am writing you this letter. Besides, it helps to pass the time.

Because of course I shall wait for Dorothea. I have a feeling that tonight she will come. This time when she beckons I shall obey her. I ought to have done so before. No one will see me going, there's a thick river-mist tonight, and I've slipped down and unlocked a side door—a little-used one that very few people know of. I only know of it because I saw Dr Braceman use it—poor man, I feel badly about him. Two suicides in a fortnight won't be very pleasant, but Tessa's was a dreadful mistake. I was the one Dorothea came to summon—I told Dr Braceman that. He didn't even bother to dispute it, just said he rather thought I might be right.

Don't let Jim marry anyone awful, and remember, I hope he marries you. I've written to him and I shall leave that letter with this one. God forgive me by blessing him—and you.

Ah—it's dark now, and I can see Dorothea. Her head and shoulders rise above the mist. The mist makes everything eerie and silent. Tessa's room is still empty. You and Jim and even Dr Braceman are all so terribly far away. And now Dorothea lifts her hand and beckons.

Forgive me, dearest Clarissa, and goodbye.

Ever your loving sister,
Julia

London,
Sunday, 31st July

Dearest Clarissa,

I don't know whether you'll ever get this letter. Jim thinks I shouldn't write. But that's only because he's afraid it will upset me, whereas actually I'll feel worse if I don't. A ghost can be exorcized, but the only way I can lay Dorothea's is by telling you about that night.

Of course I know you know it all already, but you can't know just what I felt as I crept downstairs, scared all the time of what I was doing and yet more scared of being stopped. I crossed the hall. The side door was still unfastened. I opened it. The mist struck chill as the grave. I could see the tops of the yew-hedges and the trees and stars above them, but everything below that was blotted out. There was no sign anywhere of Dorothea. I shut the door and knew I was utterly alone. There was nothing between me and the next world, and the next world had sent its emissary to this.

I began to walk towards the formal garden. My feet did not seem to touch the ground, yet my shoes were soaked through in no time. The yew-hedges too were wet. The mist had filled all the interstices like cold wet fibreglass. Everything was more solid, yet insubstantial. I never heard Dorothea approach.

Then, all at once, she was at my elbow. She did not look at my face, but she took my hand in her cold, damp one. All the time she was looking towards the lake. I could hear her skirts rustle as she moved beside me. The lace cuffs of her dress tickled my flesh. Her hair, which was ashen, clung damply against her temples. Her face was expressionless. And pale! I've never seen such whiteness, except on an alabaster tomb. It was as if a monument had come to life and yet was still a statue. I can't imagine a more terrifying presage of doom.

Dorothea didn't hurry, but she moved surely. She led me up and down and in and out as if we were treading a maze through the formal garden. Before long I was completely lost. She took long steps—I had to trot beside her— yet she wasn't much taller than I. She never once looked at my face or spoke to me, but I reminded myself that she was spirit and I was not yet dead.

All at once we were at the end of the formal garden, where the ground slopes down towards the lake. It's a long, steep slope, and that night it was filled with whiteness. Dorothea's grip tightened on my hand. Without speaking, she began to run forward, dragging me with her—she was strong. Faster and faster we ran through the wet grass, breasting the mist which lay like steam above the lake.

I could not think. I could only obey my body, which in turn could only obey her will. Suddenly she let go of me, but I went on running, impelled by my own momentum if nothing else. I ran blindly towards the lake waiting to receive me, or perhaps I had already drowned, for I heard Jim's voice, felt his arms around me, shaking me, calling my name. He caught me to him, but I was still bent on running. I tried to break away, when from the mist behind us there was a shout and a scuffle, and suddenly a terrible cry.

'What is it?' I asked. Jim said very calmly, 'Suppose we go and see?' I touched him. He was real and warm, not ghostly like Dorothea. I said, 'I thought you were in New York.' 'Dr Braceman thought I should come home again,' he answered drily. And added, 'I do, too. And here is your guardian angel.' A shape loomed out of the mist.

It was Dr Braceman—and Dorothea. I thought this time I was really mad. 'Were we right?' Jim said to Dr Braceman, who nodded. 'Then we'd better let Julia see.'

Dorothea was lying face downwards in the wet grass. Her arms were shielding her head, as though she were trying to burrow beneath the earth's surface. Even I could see that she was flesh and blood.

'You'll have to help me turn her over,' Dr Braceman commanded. He smiled at me. 'Don't be frightened, Julia. I'm quite real. I didn't go as far on my week-end as I allowed you to imagine. In fact, I never left here.'

Between them, Jim and the doctor had Dorothea pinioned. They forced her—none too gently—to her knees. Jim seized her hair, and his hand came away covered in greyish powder as he forced her to hold up her head.

Looking at me was the face in Aunt Sophie's photograph
—a face contorted with hate beneath a chalk-white make-up
that no longer concealed the features. Clarissa, for the first
time I saw *you*.

Jim took me away from Combe Tracy. Dr Braceman said
there was no point in my continuing my stay. Now that my
'evil sister' (his words) was safely taken care of, he thought
I'd recover fast enough. He added that I must try not to hate
you, since you'd been unhinged by jealousy ever since Jim
had passed you over in favour of your drab little sister. I had
come between you and him.

Even now, Clarissa, I can't believe you meant murder,
though no one else has any doubt. Dr Braceman says the
whole scheme was carefully calculated, even to making sure
Jim went to New York. With him out of the way, I'd be at
your mercy—as I should have been, if Dr Braceman hadn't
caught on. It's odd to think he kept using the intended
victim as the go-between, to keep you informed of his plans.

Jim says I shan't be called on to give evidence, since Dr
Braceman doesn't think you'll come up for trial. In the first
place because you're unfit to plead at present, and in the
second because he doubts if yours is an indictable offence.
So we've changed places dramatically, Clarissa, and you're
the one behind a window with bars; which is why I said
when I began this letter that I doubted if it would ever get
to you.

Nevertheless, whatever Jim says, I shall send it. It's
strange, but I've never made my own decisions before. But
then, I haven't been so happy for a long time, certainly not
since the day I tripped on the stairs. Because everyone agrees
now that I *did* trip over whatever it was you put in my way.

That was your first attempt at murder, wasn't it, only unfortunately for you, I survived.

I have kept my best news till last: there's going to be another baby. Jim is as delighted as I am, though he still gets angry when he thinks of how you claimed he made a pass at you. He calls that the wickedest of your lies!

I can hear him coming. I must end this letter, except that I can't think how. But habit will make me end with the usual subscription,

Your loving sister,
Julia

A Scientific Impossibility

Slingsby was the first arrival. The fact did not disconcert him in the least. If one was going to serve on these scientific committees, one might as well make a job of it. That was Slingsby's attitude in everything. On the whole it had served him pretty well. At thirty-two to be on the Publications Committee of the Ecological Advisory Council was an achievement, even though internal politics had played their part. Basically, Slingsby knew he was there because Miles Crabstone wanted him, and Crabstone, after all, took the chair. They were both zoologists, whereas the F.R.S.—no one thought of Sir Jeffrey as anything other—who was vice-chairman, had started life as a botanist. Of course Sir Jeffrey was what Crabstone called a spreader; he had trespassed into others' territories; 'taking the broad general view' was what he called it—an invitation to sarcasm that Crabstone could seldom resist.

Nevertheless, the F.R.S. was a party to be reckoned with. Crabstone had not had it all his own way. When, at the last spring-clean and general turn-out, it had been agreed to appoint to the Committee two younger men—'fellows who will show us how ecology is shaping', as Sir Jeffrey put it— it was a foregone conclusion that one of them would be his nominee. To be exact, he had put up two candidates for the two vacancies, but Crabstone had outsmarted him. At the last minute he had put forward Slingsby, his own candidate, and had succeeded in getting him in. But the F.R.S.'s other candidate was adopted. Thus the balance of power was studiedly if precariously maintained. The independent, and therefore too often the deciding, factor was George Wilkins, the second Committee-member to arrive.

As a soil conservation expert, Wilkins considered himself outside both camps, although in practice he sided with Crabstone, whom he regarded as the better scientist. He was not alone in this judgment. The F.R.S. had been elected before the war; he had an alphabet after his name, sat on strings of committees, but few people could remember what his Fellowship was originally for. He was Sir Jeffrey Caldecote, the distinguished biologist—a tag as flattering as it was imprecise, but 'taking the broad general view', as Crabstone quoted with asperity, it was as informative a description as they were ever likely to get.

Having greeted Slingsby, Wilkins was fussily divesting himself of his outer garments, which included his old college scarf, whose wearing was one of his minor affectations designed to show that he was young at heart. He was actually nearer fifty than forty, and had twice been disappointed of a chair. He showed in consequence a slight cynicism whenever advancement was mentioned, as one aware that merit was not the key.

'Well, Alan—' he turned to fish out an agenda, which he flourished under Slingsby's nose—'what d'you think of that?' he demanded.

'No comment,' Slingsby said.

'No comment? That's a good one. Almost as cryptic as the last item—A.O.B.'

'Isn't that usual?' Slingsby queried.

'Come off it, Alan. You needn't take that line with me.

You know what A.O.B. signifies this time. It's the year's greatest euphemism, I should say.'

'You're getting so literary, George, that a mere scientist can't follow.'

'Rumford's paper, man. It's coming up for consideration today.'

' "Consideration" strikes me as a bigger euphemism. You know as well as I do it's no good.'

'And you know as well as I do that Crabstone for once is on the wrong tack. We'll be the laughing-stock of Europe if he turns this paper down.'

'Hardly that. It's conclusions are so tentative.'

'But it's a revolutionary line of research. Can't you see, Alan, that's the crux of the matter? Here at last is someone doing something new. And instead of encouraging it, welcoming it, what does Crabstone want to do? Reject it and wait for something more conclusive, although Rumford says it will be years before he has the necessary data to hand.'

'Isn't that Crabstone's point—that this is a premature publication?'

'Of course it is, but he can't see wood for trees. Without the co-operation of overseas workers, how is Rumford to continue his research? And their co-operation won't be forthcoming unless they know what he's up to, which means he'll have to publish something first. He pays us the compliment of offering it to us, and Crabstone, who hasn't read anything like it previously, wants us to turn it down.'

'No. He merely returned it to Rumford for clarification and said he wouldn't recommend acceptance without. That seems to me entirely reasonable. What's all the fuss about?'

'I happened to see Rumford at the International Congress, and he told me he wasn't going to back down. He's re-submitting the paper in its original form at this meeting—and he's got the F.R.S. to agree.'

Slingsby whistled. 'So the F.R.S. is standing sponsor. I begin to see what you mean.'

'A.O.B. could mean the dissolution of this Committee. Unless one of us can nip in between.'

'And be crushed between opposing scientific bodies? Count me out,' Slingsby said hastily. 'I don't even remember the subject of Rumford's paper. Something about bird migration, wasn't it?'

'That's right.'

'Not exactly up your alley, is it?'

'Meaning——?'

'I'm surprised to find you so partisan.'

'My dear Alan, we may live in an age of specialization, but that needn't prevent us from recognizing that all science is basically one.'

'I see. "Taking the broad general view." '

'Oh, I admit the F.R.S. overdoes it, but it's not his theory that's at fault.'

'So you've been improving yourself by boning up on bird migration?'

'Don't you believe it!' Wilkins said with a laugh. 'What interests me is that here is something revolutionary.'

'No, George. There have been many other workers in the field.'

'Yes, but not this particular aspect, and none so out-standing as Rumford.'

'Is Rumford outstanding?' Slingsby asked.

'Not if you're one of those who dislike him.' Wilkins's voice made clear his opinion of such. 'But you've got to admit that he's at least outstanding in the sense of being conspicuous. You wouldn't take Rumford's for just a face in the crowd.'

No, Slingsby reflected, you wouldn't. He was far too handsome for that. Too well-dressed, too full of man-of-the-world assurance—very different from the popular idea of a scientist. Besides, Frank Rumford was an Honourable, and his father had been extremely rich. His choosing to read science had seemed at first a dilettante's foible and no one had expected that his interest would ever persist, let alone prove equal to acquiring him a doctorate and a position at a London college in research. This research had been conducted under the aegis of the late Professor Higginbotham, whom Rumford had assisted from time to time.

Nevertheless, at some point in this exemplary *curriculum vitæ*, the rumour began to spread that Rumford was 'unsound'. No one knew how it originated, but in scientific circles it gained ground. In the two years since Higginbotham's death it had been in abeyance; Rumford, indeed, had been lying very low. His paper, modestly entitled *Some New Factors Influencing Bird Migration*, was the first independent research he had produced. Particular importance therefore attached to its publication, which had so divided the Ecological Advisory Council. Surprisingly, Wilkins, who had voted against the paper in April, seemed to have undergone a change of heart.

'So I take it you'll be voting against Crabstone?' Slingsby asked sadly.

'My dear Alan, what else in conscience can I do? Much as I respect Miles, I believe his prejudice against Rumford has blinded him.' He added unconvincingly: 'Of course I may be wrong.'

'You are wrong,' Slingsby said with unexpected firmness. 'We'd do better to stay clear of this. It's very startling, but as Crabstone pointed out, it's a scientific impossibility. All the same, if it comes to a vote, I bet you win.'

'What makes you think that?' Wilkins asked, surprised and flattered.

'Brian Fox,' Slingsby replied. 'I shall vote with Crabstone, which makes Fox the deciding factor. A pound to a penny he'll come down on your side.'

Brian Fox, Slingsby's junior by four years and the youngest member of the Committee, had pursued an erratic career. He had taken a brilliant first and followed it with a severe nervous breakdown. His temperament was one of extremes. Like Slingsby, he was of middle-class origin, but he lived in a state of perpetual revolt. A repressively religious background had made him proud to be an atheist.

Between Fox and Slingsby there existed rivalry, but also a certain camaraderie. They were both relatively inexperienced in the ways of committees. Their views were invited but all too often ignored. They were alternately united against the older men and divided behind them. Neither would yield the other pride of place.

Wilkins had not previously given much thought to Fox, whom he regarded as a cipher, but he was none the less gratified at the prospect of his support. With three to two in favour of Rumford's paper, the decision was virtually in the bag—a salutary lesson for the impatient and autocratic Crabstone, who was inclined to regard the Committee as a rubber stamp. Wilkins had often longed to see his chairman come a cropper, although he knew he was not the man to bring him down. All the same, it was exciting to think that if Fox voted correctly, Crabstone's discomfiture might be at hand . . .

'Where is Brian?' he demanded irritably. 'He's usually here before anyone else.'

'Perhaps his train's delayed by the fog,' Slingsby suggested. 'The papers said it was going to get thick.'

Wilkins frowned in annoyance. It was essential that Fox should arrive, for if he did not the Committee would be evenly divided and Crabstone, as chairman, would have the casting vote. And only three days ago Wilkins had heard via the scientific grapevine that there would shortly fall vacant a Cambridge chair. At once his whole being was concentrated on obtaining it—Rumford's paper was simply a means to that end. One would be expected to show awareness of research in other branches; championship of Rumford's unorthodoxy might help . . . And with two undergraduate sons and a daughter who wanted to read medicine, money was becoming an urgent problem, for neither he nor his wife had private means.

Wilkins gazed from the door to the fog-smeared windows, and back again to the door. As though conjured up by the intensity of his anxiety, Brian Fox dutifully appeared.

He had been hurrying, and was in consequence more dishevelled than usual—and he seldom attempted to look neat. Yet his was not the nonchalant dishevelment of Slingsby, but rather the self-conscious slovenliness of a schoolboy summoned unexpectedly before the Head. Fox's socks, one felt, would always have been round his ankles, and his cap put on askew.

'Had a lousy journey?' Slingsby asked sympathetically. 'Or wasn't the fog too bad down your way?'

Fox looked at him as though the question were in a foreign language. 'I came up this morning,' he said.

He said it as though it had significance.

'Been in the lab?' Wilkins asked.

'Hell, no. He's been on his knees in St Benedict's,' Slingsby said lightly. Between them, Fox's atheism was a standing joke.

For once, however, the habitual banter failed to register. Fox looked from Wilkins to Slingsby uncertainly.

Slingsby noticed it and asked quickly: 'What's the matter? You look as if you'd had bad news.'

'I have.'

'I'm sorry, Brian. What's the matter?'

Fox looked at his colleague. 'You mean to say you haven't heard?'

'Heard what, man? Don't make such a mystery.'

Fox drew a copy of *The Times* from his pocket.

'I'm sorry to have to tell you, Alan. Crabstone's dead.'

Wilkins's reaction was incredulity. 'But I saw him only last week!'

'*The Times* says "very suddenly".'

'I didn't know you were an Establishment man.' An irrelevancy was all Slingsby felt he could trust himself to utter. Even so, grief and shock made his voice unintentionally harsh.

'I don't take *The Times* as a rule,' Fox said, colouring. 'But this morning there wasn't much left——'

'May I see?' Wilkins interrupted.

'Yes, of course. How stupid of me! As I was saying, I don't usually take *The Times* . . .'

Fox's explanation tailed off into silence. The others were

not listening, anyway. Slingsby was peering over Wilkins's shoulder. Fourth down in the 'Deaths' column, the following notice appeared:

> CRABSTONE. On November 27th, very suddenly, at his home, 2 Dryden Place, Miles Crabstone, aged 55, dear husband of Lætitia and Professor of Zoology in the University of ——

There was no mistake. All the details were correct, even down to the spelling of Lætitia and the omission of Miles's detested second given name. The age too was accurate—although no one would have believed it. Slingsby was appalled to find himself near tears. It seemed impossible that Crabstone of all men could have died on them, could have abandoned projects which in some cases were hardly begun. For the past ten years—ever since he had started research work—Crabstone had towered above him; not just physically, but as his superior in every way. Now, suddenly, there was only a vacuum; there was no one to look up to any more. And the shock was all the greater in that he had never been conscious of revering Crabstone, who had simply been teacher, senior and friend. Why, damn it, Slingsby thought with belated comprehension, damn it, I *loved* the man.

He had a sudden longing to get out of this committee-room, away from that long narrow table and its attendant lifeless chairs, away from the soft, foggy greyness of November and into strident sun and warmth. He wanted to be able to tell Peggy, his wife, what had happened. She had liked Crabstone, and Lætitia too. And ought he to call on Lætitia Crabstone, or would a note of condolence do?

His meditation was interrupted by Wilkins. 'Poor old Miles. I wonder what finished him off?'

'A coronary,' Slingsby suggested.

'Probably. Or a stroke.'

'Or it might have been an accident,' Fox hazarded. 'There are so many things it might have been.'

It was enough to make the most conscientious atheist apprehensive. There was no knowing when death might strike. So many deaths, and all of them leading to a judgment—and who except the saints emerged unscathed from that? Vistas of a Purgatory he believed he did not believe in opened up before Brian Fox's atheistic eyes. It could surely do no harm to pray that the dead might have it easy, for who knew the state of another's soul?

He pulled himself together. His mind was slipping (as it always did when confronted with sudden death) into the mould it had been cast into in childhood. He must resist this tendency to infantile regression. Was he not a scientist?

It was Wilkins, as usual, who returned to the point at issue. 'Can we have a meeting without Crabstone?'

'You mean we should call it off out of respect?' Slingsby said.

Wilkins did not mean this, but he did not wish to say so. 'What do you think?' he asked.

'I think we should go ahead because Miles would have wished it. He was always one for getting things done.'

'I quite agree,' Wilkins said heartily. 'Only sometimes people's feelings . . . you know . . .'

'What about the F.R.S.'s feelings?' Fox objected.

'We'll see what they are when he arrives.'

'*If* he arrives,' Slingsby corrected. 'He may have forgotten the day.'

The proviso was less preposterous than it sounded. Not only was the F.R.S.'s memory getting poor, but he had a marked disinclination for anything approaching disagreement. It would not be the first time that failing memory or poor health had enabled him prudently to turn tail.

The question of whether he would turn up was therefore pertinent. Wilkins recognized it at once. 'How's the fog?' he asked, seizing on the likeliest excuse to be put forward.

'You can bet it will be bad wherever Sir Jeffrey is.'

'There are many things that my presence might conceivably worsen, Slingsby, but I fail to see why fog is one of them.'

They all turned as the F.R.S. came towards them, unwinding the muffler from the lower part of his face. The gesture was curiously symbolic, for his face was immensely long. It fell away below the eye-sockets into deep leather pouches, with swags of jowl along the jaw-bone and chin. His voice, though not resonant, was carrying; it was as dried-out and desiccated as his limbs, which emerged from the concealment of shabby garments into a pair of knuckle-cracking, knotty hands.

Had the old boy really meant to cross swords with Crabstone, Wilkins wondered, or had he come, despite the fog, with exultation in his heart—exultation at the longevity that had made of him an elder statesman among scientists, while Crabstone, a prime minister, was no more. The unfairness of it overwhelmed Wilkins; it was the cruellest kind of trick. He hoped at least that Crabstone's dependants would not suffer, although of course there was only the wife—the widow now. She was not the sort of wife he would have expected from Crabstone: too physically fine-drawn and over-bred; yet she had complemented his vigour and robustness. It was sad that they had no child. Or was it? Children were an expensive item. His own three needed more than he possessed. State aid took no account of food and clothing, fares, pocket-money, holidays, all the rest. There was only one hope, and that was more money immediately. He simply had to get that Cambridge chair. But there had been no need for Miles to go and die on him . . . And yet, of course, it was providential that he had. With Crabstone gone, the paper would be certain to be accepted. 'Taking the broad general view', as the F.R.S. always put it, might prove, for Wilkins at least, to be no bad thing.

At the moment, however, the F.R.S. was in no mood to take a broad general view of anything. 'Well, Slingsby,' he intoned, 'what led you to make that—on the face of it—extraordinary remark? Have you discovered some interesting method of fog prevention and dispersal, dependent on keeping me indoors?'

He paused to allow imaginary students to chuckle. Fox dutifully took the hint.

Unabashed, Slingsby replied: 'I wish I had discovered such a method. I'd be selling it to airports everywhere.'

The F.R.S. snorted like a horse becoming impatient.

Fox said: 'I wonder if Sir Jeffrey has heard——'

He was increasingly convinced that Sir Jeffrey hadn't, but the F.R.S. rounded on him at once.

'Of course I heard! Since when have you found me deaf?' he demanded. These younger men were all the same. Gibing at those who had been eminent when they were in heir cradles. It was time they acquired manners as well as Ph.D.'s.

'I don't think Brian meant that, Jeffrey,' Wilkins interposed quickly. 'He was just asking if you'd seen——'

'He said "heard", not "seen",' Sir Jeffrey grumbled.

'If you'd seen or heard anything of Miles.'

'No. I have not.' The F.R.S. consulted his gold hunter. 'But I can tell you one thing: Miles is late.'

The late Professor Crabstone, Slingsby thought sadly. Soon he wouldn't even be that. Someone else would take his place on the Committee. In five years' time they would hardly remember his name.

'I don't suppose you've had time to glance at today's *Times* yet, Jeffrey,' Wilkins went on, 'but I'm afraid you're in for a shock.' He could see from the look in the F.R.S.'s eye that the old boy had guessed what was coming, and concluded quickly: 'I'm sorry to have to tell you Miles is dead.'

'May he rest in peace,' Fox murmured unintentionally. Slingsby looked at him in surprise.

The F.R.S. remained rigid for an instant. 'Dead!' he exclaimed dramatically, and subsided, not quite accidentally, into Crabstone's vacant chair.

Wilkins was holding out the paper. 'See for yourself,' he said.

The F.R.S. fumbled for his glasses and made great play with putting them on. These younger men had no stamina, that was the trouble. They went at things too vehemently and were dead at—what was it?—fifty-five. He found the announcement and read it through twice, slowly, trying not to betray the satisfaction it inspired. Here was he, seventy-five next birthday, and youngsters like Crabstone went and died! Of course Miles did too much and seemed to think it natural, but Nature had caught up with him in the end. And Lætitia not more than fifty. Poor Lætitia. He would have to drop her a line. Miles could not have been an easy man to live with. He often wondered if she had regretted her choice. Lady Caldecote would have sounded better than

Lætitia Crabstone. He had proposed to her himself, long ago . . .

'This is a tragedy,' he said aloud.

The others murmured agreement, Slingsby more loudly than the rest.

'A great tragedy,' the F.R.S. repeated, like an actor waiting for a prompt.

Renewed agreement.

'In Miles Crabstone,' the F.R.S. began his funeral oration (for any death demanded in his view a ritual speech), 'we have lost a friend, a colleague whom we valued. There is not a man here who was not proud to shake him by the hand. We are all the poorer for this inroad into our Committee. We shall miss him. We shall miss him very much.'

He bowed his head to indicate that the oration was over.

Fox nudged Slingsby. 'Short and sweet, but not too bad.'

'Mark Antony's was better,' Slingsby retorted.

We shall miss him. We shall miss him very much. He closed his eyes in an unsuccessful effort to recapture Crabstone's features, and opened them to find Wilkins regarding him with concern. Wilkins knew Slingsby's affection for Crabstone; he did not want to make things too hard for him.

'Would it be a good idea, Jeffrey,' he suggested, 'to postpone our meeting today?'

'Why should we?'

'I thought as Miles wasn't with us . . .'

'What difference does it make? We have a quorum.'

What difference had Miles's presence ever made, the F.R.S. wondered. Lætitia would still have refused him, middle-aged and balding as he had been. Too honest for jealousy, the F.R.S. was none the less jealous. In a way it served Lætitia right. She was now a widow because her husband had been too prodigal of his vigour. Lady Caldecote would have been differently placed . . .

'I don't see why we shouldn't carry on with the meeting,' he continued. 'Miles would hate to feel he had been the cause of inefficiency or delay.'

Wilkins exhaled audibly. It looked as though Rumford's paper would go through. He bent to extract some items from his briefcase. 'Will you take the chair, Jeffrey?' he enquired.

The F.R.S. patted the arm. 'I have already. Well, gentlemen, shall we begin?'

Then the door opened as if there were a small explosive charge behind it, and Miles Crabstone came bursting in.

Despite being impeded by a briefcase and an unrolled umbrella, Crabstone had already divested himself of coat and hat—a tweed fishing hat of uncertain age and colour—as he strode across the room.

'Afternoon, Jeffrey.' He nodded to the others. 'Sorry I'm late. It was difficult to get away.'

Crabstone always found it difficult to get away; so many people wanted things from him—advice, opinions, interest, patronage. He stopped, aware that they were all staring at him.

'What is it? Do you think you've seen a ghost?'

'Just about,' Slingsby said, beginning to grin broadly. He had read of this kind of hoax.

'We thought you were dead,' the F.R.S. said reprovingly, as though Crabstone should apologize for being alive.

'Why should I be dead?' Crabstone asked in amazement.

'*The Times* announced that you were.' Wilkins, to the point as usual, held out the paper, his finger marking the spot.

Crabstone snatched it, and demanded a moment later, 'Who on earth put this thing in?'

'No one here,' the F.R.S. said pompously. 'I hope you're not accusing us?'

'Some student's idea of a joke, no doubt,' Wilkins suggested.

'More likely wishful thinking on someone's part.'

It was Crabstone himself who made this last proposal. He obviously did not care, though he observed thereafter, frowning slightly, 'It's lucky we don't take *The Times* at home. A thing like this would scare the life out of Lætitia. Damn silly, thoughtless trick.'

'So long as it isn't true!' Slingsby could have hugged Crabstone, the F.R.S., Wilkins, even—at a pinch—Brian Fox.

'All the same, Miles, you'll have to find out who did this,' Wilkins insisted. 'It's going a little too far.'

'By Jove, yes. Strong disciplinary action.' The F.R.S. glared round at them all.

'Later, later,' Crabstone said with impatience. 'There are more important things to do. It's not the first time reports of a death have been greatly exaggerated, though as regards mine, I dare say that it will be the last.'

He had moved instinctively to his place at the head of the table and now stood like one nonplussed, for the chair already had an occupant. It was rare for Crabstone to be put out by anything; as a rule, he surmounted difficulties with ease. Slingsby, watching, noticed with surprise that this contretemps seemed momentarily to have shaken him. He appeared more embarrassed than Sir Jeffrey, who was already getting to his feet.

It was almost with relief that Crabstone sat down and busied himself with his papers. Slingsby wondered if perhaps he was not feeling well. That ridiculous hoax must have shaken him, but he would never admit it; he would sooner die.

Fox, who acted as secretary, produced the minutes of the last meeting, and Crabstone queried: 'May I sign?'

There was the usual mutter of agreement, and Crabstone felt for his pen. Not finding it, he displayed the same uncharacteristic agitation, feeling in all his pockets and muttering that they hadn't much time. Wilkins offered his own pen, a ballpoint, which Crabstone grasped as if it were the proverbial straw, and, pushing the book aside impatiently, leaned back in his chair, and said, 'Now!'

It was as though he gave himself a starting signal. He began to go through the agenda at breakneck speed. Accustomed though they were to his rapidity, the committee members were startled into protest.

'I can't hear what you're saying,' the F.R.S. complained from the foot of the table. 'Good diction is becoming a thing of the past.'

'I was only confirming that we turn down Butler's paper, Jeffrey. You suggested that we should last July.'

'Quite right. I knew I should agree with your decision. I just wanted to know what it was.'

Crabstone sighed loudly, and Wilkins murmured, 'Easy! I know we're late but it's not as bad as that.'

'Not for you, perhaps,' Crabstone said sharply, 'but I shall have to be off again before long.'

'If today was inconvenient, you should have said so. We might have managed to meet later in the week.'

'Later in the week would be impossible,' Crabstone said with finality. 'Now! May I take it we're agreed that Butler's not in?'

No one demurred, so he nodded to Fox to note it for the minutes, and passed on to the next item—A.O.B.

'Is there any other business?' he enquired perfunctorily.

'Yes.' The F.R.S. realized he sounded too firm. 'I wish to place before you a paper which I strongly recommend we accept. We all read it when it came in to us last April. Recently I've read it again. I refer, of course, to Dr Rumford's *Some New Factors Influencing Bird Migration*. I find it a remarkable piece of work.'

' "A remarkable piece of work" just about describes it.' Crabstone had squared his shoulders as if for a fight. 'Do you wish to propose it formally, Jeffrey?'

'Yes,' said the F.R.S. 'I do.'

Wilkins said: 'I'd like to second that proposal.'

Crabstone turned on him. 'George! you can't.'

'Why not?' Wilkins asked smoothly.

'Because Rumford's a charlatan.'

'Look here, I think you ought to be careful what you're saying.' The F.R.S. took on a pained-gentleman tone. 'You may not share my opinion of the paper's merit, but to cast aspersions like that is going too far.'

'Not in the circumstances it isn't.'

'What circumstances?' Wilkins wanted to know.

'Just a minute, just a minute,' the F.R.S. protested. 'I think you're forgetting that we ought to take a vote. The paper's acceptance has been proposed and seconded. Crabstone's may be the only dissenting voice.'

His gaze rested for a moment on Slingsby, with what the younger man felt was dislike.

'Very well,' Crabstone said. 'Those in favour?'

Hands were raised by the F.R.S., Wilkins and Fox.

'Those against?'

It was now Crabstone's turn to look at Slingsby, who obediently raised his hand.

'Three to two,' the F.R.S. said with satisfaction. 'The motion is carried, I think.'

'No, by God it isn't!' Crabstone cried in anger, 'With the only two zoologists against!' The hand still toying with Wilkins's ballpoint clenched suddenly. Slingsby expected to hear the plastic snap.

'We shall get nowhere by losing our tempers,' the F.R.S. said with maddening calm. 'I may not be qualified in zoology, but I flatter myself I know as much as many who are.'

'You do flatter yourself,' Crabstone interrupted.

The F.R.S. refused to be drawn. 'We must remember,' he went on, 'that science is more than a series of watertight specializations. We must be prepared to take the broad general view.'

Under the table Fox kicked Slingsby, who obligingly kicked him back, wishing suddenly that he could remember more of Rumford's paper and what the difference of opinion was about.

Crabstone had turned back to Wilkins. 'George, what's come over you? You read that paper last April and thought it was balls, just as I did. What's happened to make you change your mind?'

'I think we're getting too set in our ideas,' said Wilkins. 'It's time we gave the new men a break. The theory's odd and I admit the proof's not conclusive, but is that any reason for closing our minds?'

'It's not a reason for abandoning our judgment,' Crabstone declared; and added softly: 'Any more than is the prospect of a Cambridge chair.'

Scarlet-faced, Wilkins turned on him in anger. 'I don't know what you're getting at.'

'Sorry, George. I didn't mean it to sound so offensive, but I can't sit by and see you betray yourself.'

'I haven't changed my mind without a lot of thinking,' Wilkins murmured. He was speaking the literal truth.

'Think again,' Crabstone urged. 'When Rumford's exposed, his supporters are going to look pretty silly.'

'And when he gets a Fellowship, his supporters will be vindicated,' Wilkins said. He looked encouragingly at Fox, who nodded slightly. Slingsby, scowling, looked away. George was always so damn plausible, that was the trouble. The conservationist's volte-face, of whose true motive he was ignorant, was causing even him to doubt.

For doubt he did. There was nothing you could disprove in Rumford's paper. It was only his unfavourable opinion of the man, coupled with a sixth, unscientific sense that here was something phoney, that was causing him to turn the paper down. And might it not be that he was unduly influenced by Crabstone? Peggy had hinted as much, but wives, especially loving wives, were jealous creatures. He had been satisfied in his heart that he was right.

Now, however, that certainty was slipping. He turned to Crabstone. 'Miles, couldn't you explain? You must have some basis for accusing Rumford of being a charlatan. Perhaps if we knew what it was . . .?'

'I'm not sure that I can explain,' Crabstone said slowly.

'It was Higginbotham who really opened my eyes. You remember he did some experimental work himself in this direction? Well, he told me he'd proved years ago that Rumford's theory wouldn't work.'

'He never published anything on it,' the F.R.S. objected.

'What became of his unpublished material?' Fox asked suddenly.

'It was bequeathed to the Animal Behaviour Institute.'

'So anyone could have gone to their library and consulted it?'

'Yes.'

'But there's nothing to show that Rumford did?'

'On the contrary. He spent a long time in the Institute library, and Higginbotham's papers were what he read.'

'Then if the proof—or rather the disproof—was there, available to everybody, why the hell did he go ahead?'

'I did not say it was available to everyone. Higginbotham told me about it himself.'

'Well, really!' The F.R.S. had been leaning forward, straining to catch every syllable. 'I do think you might have said. Of course if a man of Higginbotham's standing has already disproved this theory, I withdraw my sponsorship of it at once. But considering that you must have known this at the time the paper was first submitted, Miles, I think you've been very much at fault. You had no call to hold out on us in this fashion—unless you wanted to make me to look a fool?'

This last was delivered with a jet of suspicion.

Crabstone said: 'No, Jeffrey, I didn't want that. When I first read that paper I was suspicious, but I didn't know until today that the theory had been definitely disproved.'

'Who told you?' Slingsby asked.

Crabstone looked at him in amazement. 'Who told me? Why, Higginbotham, of course.'

The silence which followed this remark became uncomfortable. It was broken by the F.R.S. remarking, 'Fellow's mad.' He said this to no one in particular, as though it were a perfectly natural thing to say. Then his eyes settled on Slingsby and he commanded briefly, 'Go out and get a cab.'

Slingsby was on the point of obeying, for his own thoughts had been much the same: Crabstone had been overworking and had had some kind of breakdown; for his own sake, it must be tactfully hushed up. He half rose in his seat, but Wilkins was already speaking, very quietly and a shade too matter-of-fact.

'You did say Higginbotham, didn't you, Miles?' he queried.

'Naturally,' Crabstone said irritably. 'Who else?'

'And you saw him this morning?'

'Yes. Ran across him accidentally.'

'Where?'

'I don't remember where. What does it matter?'

'It doesn't,' Wilkins said hastily. 'Was he—all right?'

'Fit as a fiddle. I told him he ought to come to town more often. Ought to be on this committee. I warned him we'd co-opt him, if need be.'

Fox could bear it no longer. 'You can't have seen Higginbotham. He's dead.'

Four pairs of eyes glued themselves to Crabstone's face to see how he would take this. His reaction was typical and brisk. 'He's no more dead than I am,' he declared roundly.

Fox's right arm gave a convulsive, involuntary movement which he just stopped from turning into the sign of the Cross.

From the end of the table the F.R.S.'s voice came,

quavering slightly. 'I went up for Higginbotham's funeral, I recall. Poor fellow! I didn't know him well, but we'd sat on so many examining boards together that I felt it was the least I could do. It rained, I remember . . . Miles, you were with us. Do you remember it too?'

'Funerals are barbaric customs,' Crabstone said sharply. 'We'd be better off without them, whatever the trick-cyclists think. I've told Lætitia I don't want any of that mumbo-jumbo. Death's the end and we might as well accept it, I say.'

'It's not mumbo-jumbo,' Fox began, but was abruptly silenced by a kick from Slingsby and a look from the F.R.S.

Wilkins pursued his patient examination. 'How did Higginbotham come to say what he did?'

'I was telling him of Rumford's paper,' Crabstone said easily, 'about which, rather surprisingly, he didn't know. In fact, I thought he seemed out of touch altogether. The most recent work he mentioned was done at least a couple of years ago.'

Unobtrusively, Wilkins wiped sweat from his forehead. Fox had gone very pale. The F.R.S.'s prolonged face had prolonged itself still further. His hands were trembling; when he clasped them the fingers cracked.

'You still need some embrocation in those joints of yours, Jeffrey.' Crabstone's eyes twinkled as he spoke. 'Higgin-botham was asking after you—I gather you've not seen each other lately. He said he hoped you'd be meeting again before long.'

'Thank you,' the F.R.S. said in a voice so hoarse as to be barely audible. 'That was extremely kind of him.'

Fox gave a little moan, but no one took any notice.

'Higginbotham was very much upset by what I told him

107

about Rumford's paper,' Crabstone continued. 'He told me he'd often had doubts about the fellow—a brilliant man, but not cut out to be a scientist. Just as well we've got an opportunity now to ease him out gently. He'll have to resign after this.'

'Not unless we can produce the proof that Higginbotham exploded his theory,' Slingsby murmured. 'And we can't take the word of a ghost.'

'For God's sake, Alan, what's come over you? Since when have scientists believed in ghosts?'

'Since this morning, apparently,' Wilkins answered. 'Miles, we've already tried to tell you, but I'll say it again: Higginbotham's dead.'

'But I saw him. I spoke to him. He told me——'

'Never mind all that. He's dead. He died two years ago. Of cancer. You went to his funeral.'

'It was certainly Higginbotham I saw this morning. There is no possible doubt of that.'

'Then you must have been having some kind of hallucination. You've probably been working too hard.'

'Wait a bit,' Crabstone said. 'I can prove it. Higginbotham didn't only tell me of his research. He told me where the documents were to prove it—the unpublished notes for the paper he didn't complete.'

Slingsby could scarcely repress an exclamation of triumph. However unorthodox his methods, it was typical of Crabstone to deliver the goods. This would certainly settle Rumford. Even the F.R.S. was looking impressed.

'Where are these notes, Miles?' Wilkins asked, still in his role of chief examiner.

Crabstone fumbled in his breast pocket.

'Here.'

He flung on to the table some untidy manuscript pages in a distinctive, well-spaced, somewhat flowing hand.

'Well? Would anyone care to examine them?' he demanded, when the silence again threatened to become prolonged.

The F.R.S. coughed. 'Perhaps as the senior member . . .' He held out his great bony hand. It was the bravest action of his life, and the least applauded. For a moment no one either moved or spoke.

Slingsby and Wilkins, on opposite sides of the table, both hesitated. Fox was muttering to himself—gibbering, Slingsby thought distractedly; the strain has been more than he can bear. He was not sure that he himself was not affected by it. His eyes seemed to be playing tricks. For a moment he could have sworn that Crabstone's fingers . . . But no, all was normal, and the F.R.S. was waiting, hand outstretched.

Before he had realized it, Slingsby had picked up the papers, which felt like any other papers torn from a medium-quality, ruled foolscap scribbling tablet, with one or two sheets of graph. They had been roughly folded, the edges not parallel. The outside sheets were grimed. They looked as if they had lain in some dusty, little-used cupboard. But they were real and palpable enough. Fox shrank back in his chair as the sheets approached him, but the F.R.S.'s hand remained steady as a rock.

He spread them out on the table and Wilkins leaned over him. Crabstone gave Slingsby a wink. It was so like Crabstone, this thumbs-up, schoolboyish gesture, that Slingsby could not help winking back. And then it seemed to him that his face froze, with one eye still screwed up. Crabstone's hand, which had never ceased toying with Wilkins's ballpoint, rested on the table only a foot away. There was nothing remarkable about it, except that he could see pen and table through the hand.

He blinked, but the optical illusion did not vanish. He glanced at Crabstone; the rest of him looked solid enough. Above the transparent hand a checked shirt-cuff protruded. Beneath the ancient, leather-bound tweed jacket, the forearm seemed flesh and blood. The F.R.S. and Wilkins were deep in the paper. Slingsby dared not catch Fox's eye. Brian was already overwhelmed by the situation; there was no sense in frightening him to death. Besides, it might be his own mind that was going—some form of withdrawal from reality. He struck the side of his chair with a force that was bruising, and realized that his palms were damp with sweat.

He risked another glance at Crabstone, and this time Crabstone intercepted it and winked again. Slingsby tried but failed to return it, and Crabstone leaned forward and whispered, 'We've got 'em on toast.'

At this moment Wilkins looked up from the paper. 'Miles, how did you come by this?'

'Higginbotham told me where to find it in his old lab cupboard, so I went along and dug it out.'

'You mean it wasn't with the papers in the Animal Behaviour Institute?'

'No, it had been overlooked. It's understandable, of course—just some dirty bits of paper in a cupboard. No one bothered to see what they were. In fact, no one had bothered to clean out the cupboard, which explains why they were still lying there. Higginbotham's successor apparently doesn't use it. It was empty save for a few clamps and flasks.'

'And no one stopped you from going into his laboratory?'

'No. The beadles acted as though I wasn't there. Didn't

even acknowledge when I said good-morning. It's just as well that I'm an honest man.'

Then Crabstone laughed to himself and added: 'Not that I am particularly honest, I suppose. I went there with intent to steal that paper, and that's exactly what I did. But I've prevented a charlatan from gaining kudos he's not entitled to and starting a few scientific false hares.'

'Rumford's theory would have been disproved sooner or later,' Wilkins said sourly. 'Other workers could do what Higginbotham had done.'

'Come, George, you're not very grateful to me, considering how I've saved your bacon. You were going to support Rumford's paper—were you not?'

Fox spoke for the first time since his defence of funerals. He addressed himself to the F.R.S., seeming almost afraid to look at Crabstone, though whether this was because he had noticed the transparent hand Slingsby could not guess.

'Are you satisfied that the theory is disproved, sir, and that this is Professor Higginbotham's hand?'

'Good questions, very good questions.' The F.R.S. nodded as though in the lecture-hall. 'I am satisfied that the hand is Professor Higginbotham's. I am—was—familiar with it, as you know. As for his results, superficially—superficially I say, mind!—there seems no doubt as to his conclusions. How do you suggest we should proceed, Miles, apart from simply turning Rumford's paper down?'

Crabstone leaned forward to retrieve the paper and Slingsby noticed with a shock that his whole forearm was transparent now. He began to feel about with his foot under the table to see if Crabstone's legs were solid, but all he did was accidentally to kick Brian Fox. Fox looked at him enquiringly and Slingsby tried to smile reassuringly. But it was a sickly, stillborn smile, for at that moment, just as Crabstone began to speak, he saw Wilkins give a start and gaze with fascinated horror in his direction. He too had noticed something amiss.

'I think you should see Rumford,' Crabstone was saying. 'Take someone with you—Wilkins, if you like—and confront him with the evidence of that paper. I'll wager he won't put up a fight.'

'You wouldn't care to see him yourself, Miles? You unearthed the evidence, after all.'

'It would be better if my name never came into it.'

Slingsby leaned forward despite himself. Crabstone's voice was as clear as ever, that peculiarly rich, ringing, booming voice, produced deep in the barrel-vault of his rib-cage and seeming to fill the room. But there was no doubt that the back of his chair was now visible through his body. He was disappearing before their eyes. And on Wilkins's face was the same look of thunderstruck incredulity that Slingsby knew was imprinted on his own.

Nevertheless, his dominant emotion was not fear but curiosity. He was a scientist first and last. Living matter—flesh and blood, bones and sinews—could not dissolve into thin air. How could a voice be produced from a disintegrating body? What became of the digestive tract? Could Crabstone eat without a stomach as well as he could apparently speak without a chest? In the hope of finding something edible, Slingsby rummaged in his pockets. Their contents as usual, astonished him. Peggy was continually grumbling; she went through them meticulously once a week. But all he could find was a cough-sweet, only lightly covered with fluff. Mutely he held it out to Crabstone, who looked down at it in astonishment.

'What's this?'

'A cough-sweet.'

'You can keep it.' Crabstone waved it aside. 'I'm surprised at you, wasting money on those things. They won't do you any good.'

Nor you, Slingsby thought, but Wilkins had anticipated him.

'Miles, are you feeling all right?'

'Never felt better. Why? What's the matter? Why are you staring? It's young Brian who's groggy, by the looks of things. Watch him—he'll go out like a light!'

True enough, Brian Fox had slumped across the table. His face was greenish-white.

'What's come over us?' The F.R.S. got clumsily to his feet. 'We're being poisoned. George, open the door. Get help. My eyesight's going. I can't see Miles any more.'

'We can none of us see him, Jeffrey.'

The F.R.S. sat down again with a bump. 'Selective toxicity . . .' he murmured.

'No, Jeffrey. It's because, with Miles, there's nothing there to see.'

'What's the matter with you all?' Crabstone's voice rang out, still booming.

Fox made the sign of the Cross.

'Have you all gone mad? Alan, will you enlighten me. You look as if you'd seen a ghost.'

'I have,' Slingsby whispered.

'Well, where is it? Come on, I'd like to see it too. I don't believe in these apparitions hysterics talk of, but I'm always willing to be convinced.'

Slingsby fatuously held out the cough-sweet to what was now an empty chair.

'Aha!' came Crabstone's voice, triumphant. 'You psychics are all alike. Let a scientist ask to see your manifestations and you say the sceptical atmosphere puts them off. All the same, I'd thought better of you, Alan. And for God's sake stop offering me cough-sweets. I haven't even got a cough.'

'Miles!' The F.R.S.'s voice whimpered suddenly. 'Miles, I can't see you. Where are you? Miles! I can hear you, and I can see the others. I don't understand it. Miles!'

Fox was reciting the prayers for the dying. 'Go, Christian soul, in the name of the Father, Son and Holy Ghost . . .'

Wilkins laid a gentle hand on his arm. 'Do you think it's appropriate? Miles was an agnostic, you know.'

'Was! I still am,' Crabstone insisted.

'No, Miles. Not any longer. You're something different now. You're a ghost.'

Crabstone's laugh, loud, ringing and hearty, seemed to re-echo round the room. Slingsby noticed that there was now no trace of what had passed for Crabstone. The voice, no longer localized, had a stereophonic sound.

'To believe in ghosts you have to believe in individual survival, and I don't believe in individual survival,' boomed the voice.

Slingsby caught the murmur of Fox's prayers. To his astonishment, Wilkins had also bowed his head. Otherwise there was an emptiness and the room seemed colder. It had a vault-like chill. A room of the dead.

The F.R.S. was the first to recover.

'Extraordinary experience,' he exclaimed. 'Wonder what psychiatrists would make of it?'

'Nothing,' Slingsby said. 'They're not going to have a chance to. We've got to keep quiet about it. We *must*!'

'And who are you to decree that we must suppress new scientific evidence?'

'We have no evidence except ourselves. And if we're the victims of a collective hallucination, as we must be, our evidence doesn't count for very much.'

'But you're forgetting,' Wilkins interrupted. 'We have evidence of a most remarkable kind. If the notes are where Crabstone says—which we can easily verify—that ought to be proof enough.'

'No, George,' Slingsby said. 'It's evidence to us, but not evidence we can make use of. Do you think Rumford would believe us if we told him how we had acquired it? Or any other scientist, come to that?'

'I suppose not. Then what are we going to tell him?'

'Tell him the partial truth: that the papers came unexpectedly to light in Higginbotham's old laboratory and were handed to one of us. He won't be in any position to make enquiries. If he does, there's nothing he can disprove.'

Fox looked at him. 'Are you denying that this—this visitation happened?'

'You tell me what to believe.'

'But it's proof that the soul is immortal.'

'Do you think it was Crabstone's soul we saw?'

'What else was it? It was certainly not his body.'

'A scientist,' observed the F.R.S., 'does not waste time on souls.'

'I'm sorry, sir, but I can't agree with you.' Fox had risen excitedly to his feet.

'Sit down,' Wilkins said. 'There are other reasons for suppressing this evidence. Have you thought what Lætitia Crabstone might feel?'

'Oh my God!' Fox said, subsiding suddenly.

Wilkins had been doodling as he spoke, filling in a black frame round the announcement of Crabstone's death in the paper, using the selfsame ballpoint Crabstone had held.

The sight got on Slingsby's nerves. 'George, must you do that?'

'I beg your pardon.'

'My fault. I'm sorry. I'm afraid we're all on edge.'

The F.R.S. felt the time had come to assert his position as chairman—if chairman he was; he was never to be entirely sure.

'I think we should agree,' he said, 'to scrub the records of this meeting. In view of the—er—circumstances, it ought never to have taken place. Brian, will you kindly destroy in our presence whatever notes you have made.'

'But Crabstone signed the last minutes,' Fox objected.

'He didn't,' Slingsby replied. 'I noticed it particularly. It was when I first began to think there was something the matter.'

Fox needed no additional persuasion. Crumpling his notes into a metal waste-paper basket, he set light to them with a trembling hand. The paper smoked, flared, and crumbled to blackened ashes, leaving a characteristic burnt smell.

Slingsby reflected that Crabstone would have been amused by this suspicion of brimstone, and felt anew the emptiness where Crabstone had been. If only Peggy were there . . . He stood up abruptly.

'Will you excuse me if I make my getaway?'

'Yes, go,' the F.R.S. said. 'We're all going. The fog's getting really thick. I shall be taking a cab to Waterloo if I can get one. Can I offer anyone a lift?' He was re-winding his muffler around him. Slingsby and Wilkins declined.

'I'd be glad of one, sir,' Fox said quietly, 'as far as St Benedict's.'

Neither the F.R.S. nor his companions displayed their feelings. Fox was evidently the most profoundly shaken of them all. And then, as they turned in a body towards the doorway, they caught sight of Crabstone's old tweed fishing hat hanging on the stand in the hall.

A Question of Time

It was Tim who noticed the picture—not because he is interested in pictures but because he is bored with conversation. While it is going on his mind wanders; so do his eyes. So also do his hands, but I wasn't sitting next to him. That pleasure was reserved for Babs.

There were six of us in Barney's flat, and it was already later than it should be. By which I mean it was later than our parents liked us to be out. But we weren't doing any harm, and we'd all left school, or nearly. As I told mine often enough, we'd got to be allowed to grow up.

Barney was actually the oldest of the lot of us. He must have been twenty at least. He only left art school last summer, but he struck it lucky almost at once. He designs textiles for one of the big makers of furnishing fabrics; hence the picture-collecting and the flat. Of course the flat's tiny and the picture-collecting pretty haphazard, but Barney says he learns as he goes along. He's always got pictures stacked against the walls, to say nothing of those that are hanging on them, and the pictures seem to change from week to week. I don't take much notice of them as a rule—I'm more interested in Barney. I certainly didn't remember the one Tim pointed out.

It was one of the framed ones, though the frame was battered. It was quite small and it wasn't hanging on the wall. Instead, it was standing on a spare coffee table, the way some people have wedding photographs. But there was nothing bridal about it; in fact it was a drawing of a monk, sort of greyish, with long pink fingers. I didn't think it was anything much.

Tim, however, had reached out and picked it up. 'Hey, where d'you get this from?' (It was like Tim to interrupt.)

'Bought it,' Barney said briefly.

'Whatever for?'

'Because I liked it.' He seemed to be challenging Tim to go on.

'Is it valuable?' Babs asked. (She is interested in money.)

Barney smiled. 'Not so far as I know.'

'But you think it might be?' asked Leo, who is much less stupid than he looks.

Barney spread his hands. 'I just don't know, I tell you.'

'Who drew it?' I asked.

'I don't know that either. I bought it in a junkshop the other day.'

'Didn't they know anything about it?'

'It wasn't that sort of shop.'

'So you don't know who it is?' asked Leo.

Tessa spoke for the first time. 'It's a friar, a Franciscan. I know the habit.'

'Isn't he handsome!' Babs said.

He was, too, now that I looked at him, in an ugly-attractive sort of way, like that film-star whose name I can never remember but who plays parts where he's always looking his opponents up and down with a measured, measuring look. If they're women he's deciding whether to bed them; if they're men he's deciding whether to fight. It struck me suddenly that it wasn't quite the expression you expect on the face of a religious. I craned over Tessa's shoulder to get a better look.

The friar was sitting down, though you couldn't see the chair because his habit hid it. There was something familiar about the way he sat. Then I remembered where I'd seen that attitude, with the right hand posed on the chair arm: there was a picture of a pope who sat like that. It was in a history-book at school; he wore red and his robe was trimmed with ermine. If he'd had a beard he would have looked like Santa Claus. But he didn't have a beard; he was clean-shaven. And our friar wasn't even that.

The artist had drawn his head in great detail. You could see the stubble on his cheeks and under his chin. He looked as if he hadn't shaved for days. His hair too was untidy; it was dark and curly like Tim's, and like Tim's too, it was rather long and matted, as if he'd had to do without a comb.

'I call it a waste for a man like that to be a monk,' Babs said, pouting.

'He may have made a lot of converts,' Leo pointed out.

'I should think he did. He could have converted me in twenty minutes.'

'If you hadn't seduced him in fifteen.'

Babs gave Tim a playful slap, and he caught her hand and held it, and began biting the back of her neck.

I looked at Barney; he showed no interest. Sometimes I wondered if he'd ever do it to me. I'd been in love with him the whole of that summer, and he just hadn't noticed me yet. Of course he hadn't noticed Babs and Tessa either, but Babs was always necking with Tim, and Tessa had a succession of young men (it was she who had brought Leo). I wondered if Barney was jealous, and while I wondered I caught his eye.

I could feel my face blushing even though there was nothing to be ashamed of. Barney affects me like that. I had an odd feeling that the friar in the drawing would also, if only he would turn his head.

I took another look at his face. He wasn't really handsome. He had the most enormous nose; and his face, when you looked close, was lined and his hair was greying. He must have been all of forty-five. I wondered why Leo was examining the drawing with such attention, and if his thoughts about it were the same as mine.

They weren't, for he looked at Barney and said suddenly: 'Whoever drew that could certainly draw. This may be quite a find.' (I should have explained that Leo and Tessa are also art students.) 'Have you had it valued?' Leo went on.

For some reason Barney looked uncomfortable. He slowly shook his head. 'I can't believe that drawing of Father Furnivall has any value.'

Tessa gave a little shriek. 'So you do know who he is!'

'Oh yes,' Barney said. 'I recognized him the moment I saw him. You don't forget a face like that in a hurry.' And he stared at the drawing in a puzzled, hungry way.

Babs drew herself away from Tim long enough to ask, 'What did you say his name was?'

'Furnivall. Father Francis Furnivall,' Barney said. 'He died in 1612, in prison—probably of torture—after being betrayed as he hid in a priest's hole.'

'In a what?'

'A priest's hole—a secret room where a Catholic priest could hide. Quite a lot of old houses have them, and they're often very cunningly contrived. The Catholic religion was suppressed in England in those days, but a few diehards kept it up, and a handful of priests ministered to these faithful. They went round from house to house, in disguise and always in great danger. Father Furnivall was one of them.'

I could believe it, looking at his portrait. He had a devil-may-care boldness in his face, as if he enjoyed and welcomed danger. I could imagine him in disguise.

Tim whistled. 'The one that didn't get away. What happened?'

'There was a young painter staying in the house. He had been engaged to do a portrait of one of the daughters, and he must have given Father Furnivall away. One afternoon a troop of horse led by the local captain of militia surrounded and searched the house. *Someone* must have told them about Furnivall and where he was hiding, for they made a bee-line for the priest's hole, the entrance to which was behind a painting in the drawing-room. Father Furnivall was discovered and dragged out.'

'What did they do to him?' Tessa asked in a whisper.

'They tried him and condemned him to death. It was irregular—as a rule captured priests conveniently died in prison before they could be brought to trial, but in a country district no one worried too much about the niceties. Father Furnivall's trial took place that very afternoon in the great hall, before a hastily summoned justice and justice's clerk.'

'I thought you said he died in prison—of torture?'

'So he did. His gaolers wanted him to talk, but he wouldn't.'

'Talk about what?'

'About other priests who were in hiding, and other houses with priests' holes. But he wouldn't speak although they promised him his freedom. So he was put to the question, to use the contemporary euphemistic phrase.'

'How do you know he died under torture?'

'There is no record that he was ever executed. What else is one to suppose?'

'He might have talked after all,' Tim suggested.

Barney shook his head. 'It would be out of character with a face like that.'

I agreed with him. Father Furnivall would never have done anything he didn't want to—and equally, he would have done anything he did. I could imagine him giving orders, but not obeying them. He couldn't have found it easy to be a priest.

'Why are you so sure it was the painter who betrayed him?' Tessa asked suddenly.

'Who else could it have been? The rest of the household were family or old and trusted retainers, all of them Catholics to a man. Whereas the painter had no ties of loyalty to bind him and wasn't a Catholic.'

'How do you know?'

Leo spoke so sharply that I was startled, but Barney went on as if he hadn't heard.

'Then there was that business of the entrance to the priest's hole being concealed behind the painting. Who but a painter would be likely to examine the picture so closely that he found the spring?'

'It's plausible, but not proven,' Leo objected.

'I tell you I know it's true!' Barney spoke with such vehemence he almost shouted. He brought his hand down flat on the table with a bang.

'All right, all right,' Tessa said pacifically. 'You two stop fighting.'

Leo muttered something that might have been an apology, and asked instead: 'What's the date of this drawing? Or don't you know?'

'I know very exactly,' Barney answered. 'It's dated September 28th, 1612.'

'How do you know? You haven't had it out of the frame,' Leo challenged.

'It was drawn the day of his arrest, and I know the date.'

'You've certainly boned up on Father Furnivall,' Babs said lazily. 'He must mean a lot to you.'

'Yes, he does.'

'Why?'

Barney again side-stepped the question. 'He was arrested just before midday, and arraigned that same afternoon. It was a golden early-autumn day. You can see how the light fell on his face as he sat there—a foretaste of the glory to come.'

'He's getting quite carried away,' Tim observed to no one in particular. He had regained possession of Babs, who said suddenly: 'I don't believe Barney bought that drawing in a junk-shop. He knows too much about it for that.'

'I did. Cross my heart. I can show you where the shop is.'

'Of course he did,' I cried. (Babs is always needling Barney.) 'Do you think he stole it, or what?'

'Or what,' she said succinctly; and Tim, before turning back to her, said indulgently to me: 'Shut up, kid.'

It's true I'm the youngest, but that doesn't make me the silliest. I discovered that long ago.

'Tim Phelps,' I began, 'if you don't leave off treating me like a baby——'

A hand fastened over my face. 'That's enough, Emily,' Barney ordered. I was so surprised I obeyed. Not that I was surprised at the rough-house; there's often a scuffle like that. No, what silenced me was that I could feel Barney's hand trembling, and when I looked at him there were drops of sweat on his face. I wondered whether the others had noticed it. I had a feeling Leo might have done.

A moment later I was sure of it. 'There's something funny here,' Leo said. He was looking very directly at Barney, who looked unhappily back. 'You bought that drawing less than a week ago. You bought it in a junk-shop. I've no doubt you got it for a song. You said yourself that the people in the junk-shop could tell you nothing about it. Yet you've already found out a great deal. Or shall we say you've invented?'

'No,' Barney said. 'Not that.'

'All right then. Suppose you tell us where you saw the portrait that enabled you to recognize this friar?'

'I don't know.'

'Because there isn't a portrait.' Leo's voice was hypnotically low. 'Then what enabled you to date this drawing so precisely? You don't just give a year; you give a day.'

'I've told you—it's the day he was captured,' Barney whispered. 'You can look it up in the *Dictionary of National Biography*.'

'But how did you know the drawing was of Father Furnivall in the first place?'

Barney's hands were shaking as if his wrists had springs in them. 'Because I drew him,' he said.

'Aha! So much for the Old Master nonsense and the obligingly unhelpful junk-shop.'

'I don't expect you to believe me,' Barney said slowly (even Tim and Babs were sitting up by now), 'but I drew Father Furnivall in the great hall as he faced his accusers. I remember it. Don't ask me how.'

'Are you trying to tell us now that you're not an impostor?'

'I didn't fake that drawing, if that's what you mean.'

Tessa, who had been examining it, looked up quickly. 'It looks pretty genuine to me.'

Leo took it from her. 'You're right. It doesn't look modern.' He turned to Barney. 'I never thought you had it in you to draw like that.'

'I haven't—not the me you see. But I made that drawing. When I saw it, I recognized it at once. Just as I remembered Father Furnivall, and the scene in the hall, and how he looked and what he said . . .' He buried his face in his hands. 'I can't stand it. It's all my fault that he's dead.'

I wanted to take him in my arms, but I couldn't with the others looking. I had to content myself with stroking his trouser-leg.

Leo said: 'Look here, I'm sorry if I made you out to be a forger, but you must admit it's pretty odd.'

'Odd!' Barney's voice rose sharply. 'I've been telling myself that all week. I must be going round the bend, or something.'

'No, no.' I took hold of his hand.

'Suppose you tell us what you remember,' Leo suggested. 'We might be able to clear things up.'

He sounded doubtful. Tessa was looking frightened. Babs had hidden her face against Tim's coat. I continued to stroke Barney's hand as he bowed his head and began, hesitantly at first, but growing bolder, to recall the distant past:

'The windows in the great hall faced westwards. There was a low raised dais at one end. That was where they sat—the captain of militia, the local justice, the pursy-mouthed scribe who acted as the justice's clerk. I can see them now—not their clothes but their faces. Pleased but decorous, like businessmen who have done a good deal.'

'Where were you?' Leo said gently.

'I was standing in the body of the hall, where all the household had been herded. I was leaning against the wall.'

He stopped. 'Now why was I leaning against the wall? The walls were reserved for soldiers, who stood all around like sentinels, their pikes drawn. They were keeping an eye on the household—one false move and they'd have struck you down. Everyone else was huddled in the middle of the room, even the women. But I was—privileged. I was allowed the wall.

'That was why I could sketch, of course. I had something to lean on. And I had my drawing materials with me—I don't know why. There was space around me, too. Neither the soldiers nor the household stood near me. I was isolated. No one would meet my eye. Or—no: that's not true. There were some who looked at me with loathing—some of the soldiers too. When I looked up from my drawing it was to catch their stares of hatred. What had I done that they should hate me so?'

'Go on,' Leo commanded. 'Describe how Father Furnivall was brought in.'

'With his feet fettered, dragged between two soldiers,' Barney said promptly. 'Either because of the fetters or because he had already been tortured, he could not stand. That was why they gave him a chair.

'The justice's clerk read out the indictment. The forms of justice were to be observed. The priest was asked whether he had anything to say, but he kept silent. The captain of militia leaned forward and struck him with his glove across the cheek.'

I looked at the drawing, and it was as though I saw the red mark spreading. I could picture how his head would jerk up and his eyes flash. Was that when he placed his right hand on the chair arm and gripped it, to help him control himself? It would have been so easy to strike back, so natural for the man in the picture, for there must have been an athletic body underneath that friar's gown. And no one ever held his head more proudly, or kept his lips more firmly shut.

'Didn't he speak at all?' asked Tessa.

'Yes. He said—I think I've remembered his words— that a greater than he had set an example of silence before unjust judges, and he would follow where his Master led.'

'Oh, good for him!' I cried. I hadn't meant to say it, but Father Furnivall's words were so exactly right—right for him, I mean, because I could just imagine him saying them and then for ever afterwards closing his mouth. Such a wide, strong, sensitive mouth—but cynical. He knew exactly what men's promises were worth. When his captors promised him freedom or threatened torture, the turned-down corners of his mouth would lift in a grim smile. But his lips stayed shut, and if he groaned under their tortures, they did not break his iron self-command.

'What happened next?' Leo asked, still probing.

'The justice cried out that he had blasphemed. The captain jumped to his feet and commanded the guards to drag the prisoner outside and hang him, but the justice's clerk intervened. He was a little, evil man who loved cruelty. He had a soft voice and a sneering laugh. He reminded the justice that the prisoner might be a useful source of information—if he could be "persuaded" to talk. King James's Secretary of State might be sorry to lose so valuable an informant—he let Father Furnivall hear that word—and gave his hateful laugh as he began to gather up his papers.

The justice nodded to the captain, who withdrew his order. Father Furnivall again sat down.

'All this time I had been sketching rapidly. The main lines were already drawn, though I had to put the finishing touches in later—that's why I drew him wearing his Franciscan habit, because I couldn't remember his clothes.'

'It was lucky you had a sketch-block with you,' Tessa said drily, 'to record this moment of history.'

I felt Barney stiffen with anger. 'I didn't have a sketch-block. I had a single sheet and that wasn't even a clean one. I'd been making drawings of hands—from boredom or for amusement—when we were all summoned to the great hall. I took the sheet of paper with me, together with some chalks and a book. I had no intention of drawing that portrait. I wish to God I never had.'

'Why?' I exclaimed. 'I think it's beautiful.'

Babs looked at me. 'You would!'

'No, honest, Barney. It's a wonderful drawing.'

'The kid's right,' Tessa said.

Barney shuddered so violently that I was frightened. 'Put it away. In a moment he'll turn his head.'

'Steady on!' Leo put a hand on Barney's shoulder. 'This is all jolly queer, I admit, but there's no need to get worked up about it. A portrait is fixed; it can't move.'

Barney shook off the hand. 'Don't you understand?' he shouted. 'He's going to turn his head and look at me, just as he did that day in the hall. I couldn't stand it then and I can't now, I tell you.'

'Why not?'

Barney took no notice and rushed on: 'He must have known where I was standing. His eyes turned immediately to mine. And although his hands were bound, he half lifted them as if in blessing. He knew exactly what I'd done.'

Tim said: 'Come off it, Barney. You've had your joke. No need to prolong it like this. I'm getting cold.' He snuggled Babs closer to him. 'Why are you so afraid of meeting the old monk's eye?'

'Because,' Barney said, 'I betrayed him.'

There was a silence.

'What makes you think that?' Tessa asked.

Barney spread his hands helplessly. 'Don't ask me. I just know it. That's why they looked at me with hate.'

'You're imagining things,' I said, though I did not believe it.

'Am I?' Barney looked down and absently stroked my hair: but impersonally, as if I were a dog he was fondling. I heard Babs begin to laugh.

As usual, Leo came to the rescue.

'Didn't you say an artist was suspected of betraying Father Furnivall? If so, wouldn't his name be known?'

'The *Dictionary of National Biography* doesn't give it.'

'Well then, what other work of his survives?'

'What are you getting at?' Tim demanded.

'An expert could compare the drawing with it and see if the same hand did both. It would prove Barney's point.'

'There's nothing known of him,' Barney said. 'Except this.' He put out a hand and touched the drawing, which was lying in Leo's lap.

'Bunk!' Tim said with unnecessary vigour. 'Come off it, Barney. You're only having us on.'

'I am not.'

' 'Course you are. What you're saying is bloody impossible. Do you think anyone's going to believe you, except wide-eyed Emily here?'

'Let her alone.' Barney sounded angry. 'And don't call me liar unless you want a fight.'

Tim stood up, pushing Babs aside. 'So it's like that, is it? All right then: I don't believe you. Do you want to settle it outside?'

'There's no need,' Leo interposed smoothly. 'We can settle Barney's *bona fides* in this room.' He looked at him. 'Can I take the frame of that picture to pieces?'

'If you want to. But what are you going to do?'

Leo didn't answer, merely turned over the drawing and began to fiddle with the back of the frame, while the rest of us gathered round to peer over his shoulder. Even Babs seemed interested at last.

Leo slit the brown paper which held in place the frame's wooden backing. The frame began to come apart. He laid the pieces on the table before him and turned to the picture itself. The paper was yellowed and brittle at the edges. Without the frame, it was obvious how rough and unfinished the drawing really was. It made its quality all the more striking; it would have stood out anywhere.

'There!' Leo sat back. 'I rather think this will prove it.'

Tim said: 'You haven't proved anything so far. The drawing isn't signed or initialled. In any case, Barney can't remember his name.'

'No, but he's remembered something more important.'

Tim looked sceptical. 'What do you mean?'

Leo turned the paper over very slowly. On the back were three drawings of hands.

The Spider

Justus Ancorwen was thirty-five years old, five feet eight-and-a-half inches, a bachelor, and moderately obese. He was a journalist (although he called himself a writer) who specialized in magazine articles on interior décor, cosy chats with well-known, preferably titled, persons in their settings, columns on wine and food. There was sometimes a distinctly patronizing tone to his articles: 'We liked the curtains caught back with a rose . . . the sole *bonne femme;*' but as it had never occurred to him that his accolades could be resented, they continued to be bestowed through the medium of the royal and editorial 'we'.

Surprisingly, he made a comfortable living out of his writing, and a small private income helped. He could afford to gratify his tastes and had no one to gainsay him. Self-indulgence was in consequence his vice. Not that Justus ever overdid things; he was fastidious, despite his bulk. He was still this side of gluttony, abstained from bread and potatoes, preferred steak rare and shied away from stout. Nevertheless, the choicest delicacies were always on his table. Like some women, his palate had to be tickled to respond. He was fond of toying with a scent, a flavour, a sensation, but having sampled it, his interest did not extend beyond. His refrigerator was always full of half-eaten bits and pieces which, twice a week, his charwoman took home.

Justus had lived alone for years, and liked it. He had a flat in Hampstead, near the Heath. It was on the first floor with two drawing-room windows from floor to ceiling and tiny wrought-iron balconies in front of each. The other rooms were rather less impressive, but Justus made sure they were seldom seen, and concentrated instead on the drawing-room—his setting—with results that were both tasteful and serene.

Serenity was one of Justus's watchwords. He disliked crisis, muddle, dirt, incompetence. He kept his home as scrupulously as he kept his deadlines. His reputation for reliability was high. It explained in part the lucrative nature of his commissions (for his writing was seldom as good as he supposed), but the magazine public being even less critical than he was, editors were eager to reserve him in advance. There was something satisfying about introducing Justus Ancorwen to someone well-known who had consented to have his home written up. One could rely on an article the right length, promptly delivered, and pleasing to subject, editor and public alike.

One evening late in August, Justus was returning from such a trip. August had been a hot, dry month, with cracks in the soil and baking sunlight; at nights the air outdoors was as warm as it was within. It was after ten, but the Hampstead streets were crowded. Outside pubs and cafés the customers lingered over their drinks. In the residential streets people sat out on balconies, terraces and porches. Windows were flung wide, and curtains for the most part drawn back.

Justus was in his usual state of smooth self-satisfaction. The visit had gone rather well. The people were titled, which had predisposed him in their favour, and they had given him lunch and tea. He had had dinner on the train back to London, and between whiles leafed through his notes. These were detailed and, he flattered himself, observant. An excellent article should result.

He was whistling a little as he walked up the steep road he lived in, but at the gate the sound was abruptly switched off. The top floor was brightly illuminated. He did not wish to draw attention to his return. It was some months since his attentions to Isabel Bishop had ended—attentions which, he now admitted, he ought never to have begun—but he still felt a certain reluctance to be reminded of her, or—even worse—to have her be reminded of him.

Not that he feared Isabel's further advances. She had amply demonstrated her pride. She neither avoided him nor sought him; she appeared to be utterly unchanged. When he had first moved into the flat she had said good morning, accompanying it with a pleasant impersonal smile; now that they were strangers again, she still greeted him, made some remark about the weather, and gazed at him with neither curiosity nor dislike. Justus found this disconcerting. It was almost as if the affair had never been, as though Isabel the aloof had never kindled into an ardour that had rather frightened him.

Justus was not unattractive to women in a cuddly teddy-bear kind of way. He was aware of this and enjoyed it, though he had no intention of being caught. Some day he supposed he would marry, just as some day he knew he must die, but both events were comfortably in the future; they did not disquiet him much.

The affair with Isabel Bishop had been different. That had cost him a number of white nights. The unwisdom of embarking on a friendship with the woman in the flat above him had not been apparent at first. It was only later, when he felt the urge to extricate himself, that he realized he could not: it would mean abandoning his lease. The lease was a long one, negotiated in his favour. He was pinned into place like a butterfly in a collection.

He was all the more grateful to Isabel for behaving in a civilized fashion, although doubtless the same mechanism operated in her case. She too was bound by agreements and solicitors' letters to a flat which she did not wish to vacate. It was in both their interests to be considerate, and Justus was aware of this. He showed his delicacy by avoiding a confrontation whenever possible, sometimes going to great lengths to give Isabel a miss.

Tonight he could see her sitting at her window, her hands resting, he was sure, on the needlework in her lap. Isabel embroidered exquisitely and was seldom without such work. Latterly, however, Justus had noticed that her hands were often idle as she sat, dreaming the dreams for which youth— even youth well-nigh past—is famous, and concentrating her unfocused gaze on whatever object she chanced to be looking at. Once or twice he had tried waving, but the experiment had not been a success. Isabel had raised a hand in a hail-and-farewell gesture, and Justus had felt relegated to nothingness.

The trouble was that Isabel Bishop had been a virgin. She had no background of experience, no sense of proportion, so to speak. What to another woman would have been simply an affair, without past or future, was to Isabel a great deal more. She confidently expected marriage, and allowed that expectation to be known. Justus, already tiring of her, became aware that she regarded him as her life mate. Thereafter his affection suffered a rapid diminution; he congratulated himself on having had a narrow escape.

Indeed, now that his transient interest was over, he

wondered what he had seen in Isabel—a big, dark girl, firm-buttocked and deep-bosomed, who failed to carry herself well. She was tall and wore flat shoes in an effort to counteract it, which enhanced her too long, too independent stride. She walked like a woman bent on demonstrating her own lack of attachments, in whom unattractiveness has become a source of pride. Not that Isabel was in fact bad-looking; with a different personality, her face and figure would have been good; she was a university librarian, she could afford to dress well—except that dressing was an art she had not understood. She bought good clothes, but she bought to last; she was out of fashion—not glaringly, but dully out of step. Justus winced inwardly at many of her outfits. Fortunately she looked much better undressed.

As he closed the gate quietly behind him, Justus kept his eyes on Isabel. She had not noticed him; he was relieved and thankful. He stole stealthily towards the house. The Powells who had the ground floor were on holiday. He and Isabel would be alone in their respective flats, separated by the width of plaster and beams and floor-boards from any communion closer than that. Nevertheless, Justus closed the front door of his own flat behind him, feeling more than usually glad to be home. He was tired; he would have a bath followed by a nightcap, followed by an early night and at least eight hours' repose. Then he remembered that he had forgotten to switch on the immersion heater; the water would be stone cold. It looked as though he would go to bed even earlier than expected, but he was far too irritable to feel consoled.

He tried the door of the sitting-room where the drinks were, only to find it locked. Justus swore under his breath, although he was himself responsible, having carefully turned the key that morning before he started out. He was exceedingly particular about burglars, and kept everything carefully locked, although since the keys were left in the drawer of the hall table, no burglar of ingenuity and experience would for long have allowed himself to be blocked. However, no burglar had called in his absence. The keys were where they always lay. Justus selected the right one, fitted it into the keyhole, and proceeded to unlock the door, leaving the key on the outside.

The room smelt stuffy as he entered. He flung the two tall casement windows wide. Outside, the warm night air was soft as feathers; somewhere, not too far distant, an owl cried. Justus stood on the balcony inhaling; the garden was moonlaced with silver below. He wondered if, at the window above, Isabel still sat with her sewing—and decided abruptly that he did not really want to know.

As though a chill had fallen on the night, he shivered, and, closing the windows behind him, came back inside. Fatigue had set his nerves on edge; it was time for that nightcap. He poured himself a drink and went to the kitchen in search of ice.

The refrigerator was full, as usual, of half-eaten titbits, delicacies that he had sampled and cast aside. Fortunately the charwoman came tomorrow; he would be glad for her to have the lot. He drew out the ice-tray and, holding it gingerly, carried it across to the tap. Then he drew back with a movement of horror and repulsion. There was an enormous spider in the sink.

Justus had an unreasoning fear of spiders. It had tormented him ever since he was a child. They appeared to him black and monstrous and evil; their presence in a room was enough to make it seem defiled. More particularly, Justus dreaded that one might get on him, its eight legs running up his flesh. He was convinced he would die if one of the bent-legged brutes should touch him; against this conviction reason was powerless. His fear belonged to the same class of instinctive horror as that inspired in other people by mice, black beetles and snakes, except that Justus rather liked mice, handled snakes (non-poisonous) with equanimity, and was not noticeably sensitive about crushing black beetles underfoot. Only spiders produced in him this peculiar terror, this inability to stay in a room where one was known to be at large, this dread even of attempting to kill one in case he fluffed it and was in turn attacked.

He had learnt, of course, to master his terror a little; he no longer screamed as he had done when a child. He had even killed spiders by dropping heavy weights upon them (he kept a stack of old telephone directories with this eventuality in mind). He could hit them with a shoe—provided his foot were not in it; but the thought of treading on one, even through a thick leather sole, turned him faint. For him, the months of August and September were months of torment, for at that time of year the spiders came indoors. At any moment a dark form might dart across the carpet and put his screwed-up courage to the test. The fact that, should one do so, he risked making himself ridiculous before others was not the least part of Justus Ancorwen's distress.

On this occasion, however, after the first moment of revulsion, he congratulated himself that he was so strategic-ally placed. He had only to turn on both taps to wash the spider down the waste-pipe, up which it had no doubt laboriously climbed.

He had once read that spiders came indoors in search of water; it would certainly explain their frequent presence in bath and sink. Now that he looked closely at this one, he saw it was near a little pool of water. Was it against the laws of hospitality to kill a guest who had dropped in merely for a drink?

The spider in the sink was a big one. Its body was not black but dark brown. Its legs were bent at an obtuse angle. It had a relaxed, almost wallowing, look. This was understandable if it had come in search of water from the drought and dust outside. For an instant Justus was reminded of a man sprawling in his bath-tub. Then, with a decisive gesture, he turned both taps full on.

The spider had barely time to bunch its legs together before the water swept them from under it. It struck out gamely, recognized that the cascade was too much for it, and was borne in an unprotesting ball towards the waste-pipe. There, in a swirling maelstrom, it disappeared. Justus ran the water for several minutes, determined to make absolutely certain that his enemy was destroyed. Normally it took no time to dispose of a spider in this way and the annihilator could afford to be brisk, but this had been a big brute and he proceeded accordingly. He was not taking any risks.

When he was satisfied that everything must be over, he turned off the taps and reverted to the matter of his drink, which he now began to feel he needed badly. He picked up the ice-tray and was preparing to dislodge the ice-cubes when a movement near the waste-pipe caught his eye. He stood as frozen as the water in the ice-tray while the spider, drenched and waterlogged, clambered forth.

It rested for a moment, clearly exhausted. Justus could almost see it give itself a shake. It moved a leg, as though making sure no bones were broken, and suddenly began to run. The transformation from stillness to movement was startling; it was doubtless a reflex of fear. In an equal reflex, Justus dropped the ice-tray he was holding and reached for the taps once more.

The spider had reached the sink-side and was trying to climb it, but the smoothness afforded it no hold. Its legs struggled frantically for purchase, but each time it slithered and fell back. Meanwhile the water from the taps was swirling round it (Justus imagined it ankle-deep), but in its corner the spider was protected from the flow's violence and able to hold its own. So long as it cowered there, the water could run for ever; something more drastic was required. After a moment's thought, Justus turned off one tap and fitted to it the short rubber hose he used for cleaning down the sink.

Against this concentrated jet of water, the spider was powerless. Again the unresisting black ball was swept towards the waste-pipe and again Justus Ancorwen drew breath. Then he became aware that the water was meeting resistance; the outflow was obstructed in some way. The sink would begin to fill, and then, with a glou-glou, the obstruction would yield momentarily and the water drain away. With each gurgled siphoning of the water, a great air-bubble rose and burst. It took Justus a moment to realize that the spider had grasped the underside of the sink-grille and was clinging on for literally dear life.

Sickened, Justus turned the hose upon the sink-grille. The bubbles rose faster now. But they rose; the spider was still living. He felt the sweat starting on his brow. If he had only had hot water, it would have been easy, and for the spider a less protracted agony at least. He deflected the flow of one tap to fill a kettle, and against the reduced cascade he saw two feeler-like legs emerging. Despite himself, Justus admired the persistence of the beast.

The kettle filled and on the gas, he once more directed the hose-jet upon the sink-grille. Something in him imagined the spider's despair as the flow redoubled after the respite. He wished to God he need not go on standing there. But someone had to direct that sink-hose. The normal flow was not sufficiently strong; it would never dislodge the spider from the sink-grille—and the spider was determined to hang on.

Behind him he could hear the kettle singing, when suddenly the intermittent glou-glou stopped. The air-bubbles had ceased to rise and burst as the obstructed water poured down the waste-pipe. The spider had been finally overcome. Relief and guilt were uncomfortably mingled in Justus: relief because the spider was no more, and guilt because never in his life had he felt such a murderer, such an evil instrument for destroying the miracle of life. The spider, by its resistance, had become personalized; it had battled bravely, although the odds were all on his side. The forces he had used against it seemed suddenly contemptible, like his fear of it, which was the reason it had died. His irrational terror had led to its slow destruction, not even to a quick and easy death. He had tortured it, buffeting its fragile body with the water, making it know fear, perhaps pain, and a drawn-out struggle for breath.

The kettle boiled over behind him. Justus seized it with shaking hands. The least he could do for what was left of the spider, to say nothing of his own peace of mind, was to make sure it did not linger in the waste-pipe. As though pouring an expiatory libation, he emptied the kettle's contents down the sink.

Afterwards he had his drink—neat—and hastened to go

to bed. He was shivering despite the whisky. He longed for warmth, sleep, darkness and oblivion. All these he found as soon as he laid down his head.

He did not know how long he had been asleep when he wakened, nor what had aroused him. It was dark. He could not even make out the window, framed between its curtains, although he could feel the night air blowing in. It was late enough for all activity to have ceased in the streets and gardens, and still a long while before the dawn. The moon had set; the street lamp outside glowed dully; a car whined up the hill in the distance and was gone.

Justus sat up and switched on the light beside him. His watch showed half past two. His room looked perfectly normal, yet he was increasingly convinced all was not well. He considered whether he had indigestion, while straining his ears for the least sound. Nothing. The silence had a heavy, wadded quality, like something in the heart of a cocoon. Nor was he afflicted with any of those discomforts which an acid stomach can cause. Nevertheless, a little bicarbonate might be helpful; it could do no harm to try.

He put on his slippers, mindful of the time of year and the risk of spiders; and wrapped his silk dressing-gown reassuringly about him until he resembled a mandarin. The bicarbonate was in the bathroom cupboard, and he had just opened the door when a sound, or rather a vibration, froze him with horror. There was someone in the drawing-room.

He supposed he must have neglected to fasten the windows. For an athletic thief those balconies would be an easy climb. And now the man was prowling about among his treasures. He must get to the 'phone and dial nine-nine-

nine. Justus had such a dread of burglars that he had frequently rehearsed what to do if one ever came. Now this recurrent nightmare was happening. And the telephone was in the drawing-room. He could not dial the police. He could only brave it out and hope that the burglar, more frightened than he was, would do a bolt as he flung open the drawing-room door.

Justus was not a physical coward, his fear of spiders apart. His heart was beating less fast as he crept down the hall towards the burglar than it had done when he drowned the spider in the sink. He moved with surprising speed and silence, having all a portly man's grace and lightness on his feet. The drawing-room appeared to be in total darkness. Outside the door Justus paused to listen and reflect.

The silence in the room appeared to equal that in the hall outside it. It seemed impossible two men could stand so still. Then, just as Justus was beginning to think he had imagined the burglar, there was a movement on the other side of the door. Again, it was not so much a movement as a vibration—as though a cat had run across the room. The district abounded in cats; it was perfectly possible that one had climbed to the balcony and got in. There might even be two cats; yes, that was even more likely; two cats at play who had bounded across the room.

Justus flung open the door and switched the light on. A draught greeted him; one of the two tall windows was ajar. The catch, always weak, must have broken; it was the sound of this that had perhaps awakened him. Dazzled by the light, Justus stood blinking in the doorway; nothing seemed to be broken or disturbed; none of his precious objects lay in pieces; he could not even see the cats. They must be lurking behind the sofa; he made a move to go and see, when an unfamiliar dark object in the corner near the bookcase suddenly attracted his eye.

Crouched in the corner was the largest spider that Justus or anyone else had ever seen. It was about the size of a coal-scuttle, black and hairy, with the lower part of its body a good ten inches off the ground. Its great legs were bent up around it like a protective fence; they were covered in bristles like a hearth-brush; the two front ones ended in claws. Justus had read once in a children's encyclopædia that, size for size, the claw of the spider is more terrible than that of the lion, and this information came back to him now, making him regret the random and unselective reading that was at once his good fortune and his curse. He imagined those claws tearing into him as he lay paralysed by the spider's venomous bite. Their poison, he recalled, operated on the nervous system; a victim could be eaten while still alive. And eaten was a delicate expression; Justus had once watched a hungry spider gorge, moving this way and that above the web-bound fly—its supper—like someone tilting and scraping the plate. Later the dry husk of the fly had been cast from the web's centre, while the spider retired to digest. Later, Justus thought, his own drained body would be abandoned, while this blood-bloated monster slept.

He dared not move, lest movement should act as a magnet and bring it forth with a flurry of its eight cat-like-sounding feet. He could not see its eyes, but he knew it was aware of his presence—by scent, or by vibration, perhaps.

Justus longed to believe that it was part of a nightmare, brought on by the events of the evening and his own dis-ordered nerves, but there was something too exact and palpable about all his surroundings; he feared the horror was all too real. And even if it wasn't, what means had he of proving it except by putting it to the test? Walking towards the giant spider, poking it . . . Justus could too easily imagine the rest.

He had read of people fainting with terror, and he wondered now if he were to be one more. He heard his own irregular gaspings and heartbeats, and felt the colour flood into and drain from his face. Only his hand clutching the door-handle kept him upright; the knuckles seemed bursting through the skin. A tremor went through his rigid, knotted muscles. And at that moment the spider moved.

It was only a little movement, but it was enough for Justus. Somehow he was outside in the hall with the drawing-room door slammed shut. The spider's eight legs blurred to a rumble of sound behind him. It stopped just in time to prevent itself being flattened against the door.

On his side Justus Ancorwen, his hands shaking, turned the key and drew a shuddering breath. He had gained a temporary safety, but he had still to think what to do next. He could dress and go out to a public 'phone-box and dial the police or the Zoo, but at three o'clock in the morning he doubted very much if they would believe him; they would be more likely to charge him with a malicious call. Alternatively, he could go in person. Hampstead police-station was conveniently near. But would they be any more likely to believe him? They might assume he was crazed without attributing it to fear. Or they might think him drunk. If only he hadn't had that whisky! How long did alcohol linger on the breath? But the truth was he did not feel inclined to risk it. Until dawn, outside help was definitely out.

There remained his friends, of which he had a number. Even so, he hesitated to ring them up. It is carrying friendship rather far to rouse a man from slumber to tell him there is a spider as big as a coal-scuttle in your flat. Justus thought he knew the kind of answers he would be given: terse, unhelpful, unsympathetic, and even downright coarse. Admittedly his friends were going to laugh on the other side of their faces later, but that did not help him at present to decide what he ought to do.

If it had been any creature but a spider, Justus felt he would have been able to cope. A lion (apart from the fact that its claw was inferior to the spider's) would have been easy by comparison. Like Samson, he would have rent it apart, and worn the pelt like an African witch-doctor; they were said to set great store by lion skins. And even if he did nothing of the kind, but merely waited until morning, at least he could wait with dignity. He would not be driven from home by his own unreasoning horror to seek any form of society, especially since the only society available was that of Isabel Bishop whom for months he had been trying to avoid.

Now that he had formulated the thought, he felt a bit better about it. Isabel was a woman; she would surely understand. It was not so long ago that she had been crooning over him as if he were a baby, and asking what he had looked like when he was a boy. Justus couldn't remember if he had told her, but for the first time he appreciated her desire to know; it argued a sympathy which he felt he badly needed. Leaving the front door of his own flat propped open, he started up the stairs on tiptoe.

The action brought back memories he would rather not have awakened. How often last winter had he crept up these same stairs. Outside Isabel's door he paused and listened. He had been accustomed to give three short rings; before the third had died away the door would be open, and Isabel waiting eagerly to draw him in. Should he do so now to assure her she need not be frightened, or would it merely serve to make her close her ears? Having once given himself away, he could not then assume a new personality. It would be no use giving a thunderous knock and shouting 'Police'.

His hesitation was ended abruptly by something running lightly over his foot. Justus leapt in the air with the agility of a ballet-dancer, though he landed without the grace. His heart was again thumping uncontrollably, and he gazed fearfully behind him down the stairs. It could only have been a spider—that tickling, feathery run. The monster must be spawning them in thousands. They would come after him. Like the rats after Bishop Hatto.

The three short rings he gave at Isabel's doorbell were the result of a reflex of fear, and it is possible that he would have gone on jabbing it indefinitely had the pursuing spiders not explained themselves away. As he moved again and felt that terrifying tickle, he noticed one fringed end of the cord of his dressing-gown trailing on the floor because he had failed to tie it securely. It was brushing lightly against his foot.

He was still recovering from this confusion when the door opened on a chain and Isabel Bishop peered out. Justus noticed mechanically that she had her hair in curlers—a habit he had forced her to abandon during their affair. The chain on the door, though not new, had not been used for a long time. Isabel had clearly reverted to type. Her voice when she spoke was polite, but guarded and distant.

'Yes, Justus? What is it? Are you ill?'

It gave no indication of her feelings, which were in the wildest tumult of hope and anger and joy. Justus Ancorwen here, on her doorstep, in the small hours? What impertinence! And how she longed to forgive her cruel, heartless boy!

She had spent months in blackening his character, but on so slippery a surface denigration refused to take. The most she could manage were one or two streaks of greyness—and in the small hours all cats are grey. She had so often dreamed of his returning, her needlework lying idle in her lap, that now that he had she believed she was still dreaming. She spoke guardedly because she feared to wake up.

Moreover, like the dreams of most romantic women, Isabel's were of the Florence-Nightingale type. Justus would be ill and she would save him by her nursing. She would look after him, blind or crippled, and be the radiance and blessing of his life. Such dreams ignore the realities of the given situation, but they are powerful motivators none the less. There was a world of wish-fulfilment behind Isabel's enquiry, which Justus, egotistically innocent, could not guess.

Instead he came out with what was uppermost.

'Isabel, you've got to help me. There's an enormous spider in my flat.'

Isabel looked at him as though she suspected her hearing. 'You rouse me in the middle of the night for that?' She omitted to tell him that she had in any case been lying wakeful. She had in fact been thinking of him.

'I know it must sound odd,' Justus insisted—he was determined she should understand—'but honestly, I've never seen anything like it. Do you think I could use your 'phone to call the police?'

'Call the police to catch a little spider?' Isabel began to wonder if he was mad.

'It's not a little spider,' Justus protested. 'It's as big as— bigger than—a cat.'

'Then it isn't a spider,' Isabel declared authoritatively. 'The biggest in the world aren't that size. I know,' she added. 'I'm interested in natural history. I always look at all the books on it that come in.'

'Perhaps you haven't got the latest editions,' Justus suggested, regretting his flippancy too late, since adverse comment on the library was to Isabel a personal affront. 'Or it might be a mutation, do you think?'

'Are you sure it didn't come from Mars?' Isabel asked icily. She made no move to open her inhospitable door.

'I don't know where it came from,' Justus said desperately. 'All I can tell you is that it's there.'

He would have invited her to see for herself but for one thing: in her incredulity she might conceivably let it out. Isabel had no fear of normal spiders; she would not take even ordinary care. And supposing it were to kill and eat her? He would incur some adverse comment in court. He might no longer be welcome in titled houses if it became known that he had behaved less gallantly than he ought.

'Isabel,' he said, with all the sincerity he could muster, 'I'm not joking—really I'm not. I woke and heard something moving in the drawing-room. When I went to look, I found this monster there.'

'What did you do?' Isabel asked, despite herself interested.

'I locked the door on it.'

'Can it get out?'

'No,' Justus said. 'I don't think so.'

'Then why have you come up here?'

'Because my 'phone is in the drawing-room.'

'You could go out if you wanted to 'phone.'

She was inexorable in her shameless stripping of his motives.

'All right,' Justus capitulated. 'I didn't want to stay down there alone.'

'Ah!' Isabel relaxed triumphantly. 'I thought it was something like that. And why should you suppose I want your company?'

'I don't suppose you do,' Justus said. 'I don't blame you. You've a perfect right to be sticky. Only I hoped that, being you, you'd understand.'

He waited hopefully for the results of this flattery, but Isabel merely smiled and said: 'Being me, I understand all too well. You've simply discovered that I can still be useful to you. That's all there is to it.'

Justus shrugged. 'If you insist on hurting yourself in this way . . .'

'What else am I to think?' Isabel asked.

She prayed earnestly that Justus would come up with a suitable alternative, something as a sop to her pride. There was nothing she wanted more than to slip that chain off the front door, but he must pronounce the open sesame first.

Fortunately Justus did not fail her.

'Look, Isabel,' he said, looking first down, then up, and then sideways, 'forget what's been between us—if you can. I'm not here to make excuses or to argue. I had no right to begin it, if you like. But since I did, and since you weren't unwilling, accept that I also had a right to make an end.'

'What about me? Don't I have rights?' Isabel interrupted.

'You also could have made an end if you had wished.'

'But I didn't wish!'

'I know. I'm very sorry. I didn't mean to make you love me, Isabel.'

'Love you!' Isabel cried, furious at this correct interpretation. 'I couldn't care less what you do.'

'Then if it's really such a matter of indifference, couldn't you perhaps open the door?'

Isabel undid the chain and held the door open in silence. Justus passed into the flat. Isabel pointed to the 'phone which stood on a small hall table. 'You'd better ring up the police.'

'I can't,' Justus admitted. 'They wouldn't believe me.'

'Any more than I do, I suppose.'

'Do you think I've made all this up?' Justus demanded.

'I think you've been drinking,' Isabel said.

'You mean you think I'm seeing pink elephants?'

'Pink elephants in your particular form.'

'It's not true!' Justus exclaimed in anger. 'Look, my hands are steady as a rock.' He held out his hands, which in his excitement were shaking, and dropped them on Isabel's shoulders to conceal the fact.

She flinched, but did not withdraw them. Justus had to do so himself. He thought he detected disappointment in her, but dismissed the idea at once. He had no wish to become involved once more with Isabel Bishop. Looking at her now, he wondered how he ever had. She seemed to him gross and unattractive, her hands and feet and body all too big. In an effort to improve her, Justus put out a hand and touched a curler.

'Must you continue to wear these?'

'I must,' Isabel said, jerking her head away from him. 'I'll look a sight tomorrow if I don't. And I no longer share your view that tonight is all that matters. If you don't like me as I am, you can go.'

He was in her power, Justus realized; this was her trump card. It was one she all too clearly meant to play.

'I do like you as you are,' he said a shade too hastily.

Isabel seemed waiting for something more.

Damn it, was she expecting him to kiss her? Justus essayed a peck. But it was so late, so unspontaneous, it was insulting. Isabel averted her face.

'You don't have to pay for your night's lodging. Don't worry, I haven't yet sunk as low as that.'

They stood glaring at each other from opposite sides of the hallway. Suddenly Isabel began to cry.

'What's the matter?' Justus asked, irritated and resentful. Trust a woman to make a bad situation worse.

'I don't know what I've done,' Isabel sobbed, gulping, 'that you shouldn't love me any more.'

Justus wondered whether to point out that he had never protested he loved her. On second thoughts, he decided to forbear.

'Look,' he said awkwardly, 'let's have a cup of coffee. There's no need for all these tears.'

Isabel stopped crying long enough to consider how to take this.

'That's my girl,' Justus approved.

She brightened up and departed to the kitchen, leaving him to regret the ill-chosen phraseology of his remark. Whichever way he moved, he seemed entangled, as though he were a fly caught in that gigantic spider's web. He listened, but no movement could be heard through the floorboards. The creature had all its species' ability to lie low. He imagined it crouched in some dark corner, its attention focused on the door.

It was partly this immobility of spiders that Justus found so frightening. There was no indication when they would move, no muscles flexed and tautened, nothing even to signify the direction in which they would run. He had been told as a child that they never ran towards you—'they're more frightened of you than ever you are of them'—but he had disproved this theory on numerous terrifying occasions, each more distressing to him than the last.

He was almost relieved to see Isabel return with the coffee. He noted that she had removed the curlers from her hair, which now fell dark and snake-like about her shoulders, giving her a witchlike air. He had never noticed before that there was so much hair about her, but perhaps he was unduly sensitive to hair tonight. The thought of the giant spider's black, bristling body produced in him a shudder of dislike.

His cup rattled, spilling coffee into the saucer.

'What is it?' Isabel asked.

'I was thinking of that horrible spider.'

'You're not still harping on that?'

'You haven't seen it,' Justus answered.

'That's easily remedied.'

'No. You mustn't. It might attack you.'

'I should simply tread on it.'

'But Isabel, it's too big. You *must* believe me.'

'I'm sorry, Justus, but I don't.'

'There would be no point in my inventing such a story.'

'You could have had a nightmare, couldn't you?'

'I could, but I assure you I didn't. The creature is real enough. If I were superstitious I should say it had come for vengeance.'

'What are you talking about?'

Hesitantly, Justus told her about the murder of the spider he had found in the kitchen sink. The recital upset him. The creature's death had been so prolonged, so horrible. It did not do to let oneself dwell on it.

Isabel sat with eyes downcast while she listened. She had picked up her embroidery-frame. A needle threaded with coloured silk lay ready. She began idly to work it to and fro. Backwards and forwards went the needle, unhurried, patient and well planned. A corner of the design was taking shape already. It was like watching a spider at its work. The simile stopped Justus in mid-sentence.

Isabel looked up. 'Do go on.'

'I forget where I was,' Justus muttered.

'You were about to pour a kettle of boiling water down the sink.'

'That's right,' Justus agreed, 'so I was. So I did, I mean,' he corrected. 'That put paid to the spider all right.'

'Until your guilty conscience aroused you. Strange. I've never known you have a conscience before.'

'You're being a bit hard, surely.'

'Am I? No, Justus, I think not. What you don't like, you've no use for. All you want is to have it removed from your sight. Like those bits of half-eaten food in your refrigerator.'

Justus hoped she was not going to carry this comparison too far. There was no telling where it might lead them. He must try to distract her again—and with Isabel he knew of only one way to distract her.

He put out a hand as if absently and allowed it to caress her hair. It was going to be a long time till morning. He was not sure how many more hours like the last he could bear.

'You must be feeling more like yourself,' Isabel said drily. But she did not jerk her head away.

'It's the good effect you have on me,' Justus murmured— the only thing he could think of in reply.

They sat in silence for some minutes while Isabel embroidered and Justus mechanically went on stroking her head. The gesture was soothing to him, though not to Isabel, who was hoping for something more. She continued to insist to herself that Justus was not worth the having— but this fact was accepted by her head, not by her heart, which, as always, beat uncomfortably fast in his presence— though not so fast as to make her wish him to depart.

Isabel's instincts had always been primarily maternal. A man was the giver of children—in the literal sense, a mate. She therefore thought essentially in terms of marriage because this was the way she had been taught. She had seen herself as the mother of Justus's children, above all, of Justus's sons. It had been a cruel awakening to discover that whatever she herself might desire, she was not desired in her turn. And therefore her desires must remain unsatisfied. Isabel felt this to be bitterly unfair. Like being required to pass an examination in Old Testament history before one could take a course in electronics or child welfare. She hated the advantages which Nature had so generously bestowed upon the male sex, while at the same time feeling herself superior to men. And superior to Justus Ancorwen in particular, who was frightened by a little spider in his den.

And now he was here beside her. Not as closely as he had been in the past, perhaps, but still, it was to her he had turned when a nightmare overwhelmed him. She allowed herself to forget that there was no one else in the house. Not for a moment did Isabel believe Justus's story, especially now that she had heard what led up to it, but she felt a great tenderness for him, as for a child who has been frightened. She longed to be able to comfort him.

'You know,' she said, 'this giant spider is all nonsense. I never heard sound of it.'

'That doesn't prove anything,' Justus answered.

'But I heard you slam the drawing-room door. I was awake anyway,' she added, 'and I heard all your movements downstairs.'

She had in fact wondered if he too were wakeful and if it was through thinking of her. He might have regretted ending their association and be seeking a means of reopening the affair.

'If there was really a spider in your drawing-room,' Isabel persisted, 'a spider as big as a cat, I should have heard it when it ran across the room towards you. I can hear most of what goes on in your flat.'

Justus was half convinced by her logic. He allowed it to show in his face. The room was warm, the coffee excellent. He began to forget his fear. On the face of it, his story was ridiculous. He could not blame Isabel for disbelief. Spiders, as she said, simply did not grow to such proportions; but his imagination did. That horrible business of murdering the spider had undoubtedly upset his nerves. At the end of a tiring day and on top of a good dinner, it had been just too much for him. He had had nightmares before, though of a different nature (usually he dreamed that he was trapped), but it was not surprising if, after such an experience, the subconscious manifested itself in other forms. Depend upon it, it was his imagination. He had been brought up in his mother's belief that he was highly strung. The giant spider would prove to have as innocent an explanation as the small one which he had believed was running over his foot.

Instinctively he relaxed and let his arm slide downwards. Isabel was not so bad after all. No beauty, and a little too intense for comfort, but a woman in her reactions—and in her curves. She had a woman's earthy common sense, too.

No giant spiders for her! Every man at times required such a corrective. Perhaps he had been wrong in not pursuing their affair. Not, of course, that he would marry Isabel, but it ought to be possible to string her along. Some heaven-sent excuse would surely arise to prevent their union. If not, one could be manufactured here on earth . . .

'You're very affectionate,' Isabel remarked, snipping her silk thread. Her body moved under his hand.

'Ah—' Justus expressed many emotions in that long-drawn-out monosyllable—'you're very attractive, my dear.'

'You surprise me,' Isabel said. Her heart was beating faster and she knew her colour was rising. But she was determined this time, to hold out. She had to make sure of what she wanted. There must be no more mistaking the means for the end.

Justus put out a hand and turned her face towards him. 'Do I surprise you, Isabel?'

'Very much, if you really mean I am attractive. Why in that case did you break things off?'

'I panicked,' Justus said truthfully. 'I didn't want to go too far.'

'You mean you didn't want to marry me,' Isabel persisted.

Justus turned away his head. His profile was one of his best angles and he knew it. If he held his head up, his double chin hardly showed.

'Isabel,' he began, speaking softly, 'must you drag marriage in all the time?'

Isabel started to say yes and reconsidered. To her, marriage was the inevitable prelude to a child, but it was the child she wanted rather than the husband. She did not really want Justus around. There were, she knew, unmarried mothers who had deliberately chosen their lot. One could always move elsewhere, become technically a widow; one was as likely to be believed as not. As for Justus, he would be thankful to be rid of her; if not, she must certainly contrive to be rid of him. A smile transformed her lips as a solution struck her. For an instant her face had a predatory, lupine grin.

She felt no hesitation, for what did she owe Justus? She was about to make final settlement of account. He would not, she was sure, return to her afterwards, for she would humiliate him so that he would not be able to hold up his head.

'I'm sorry, Justus,' she said, sounding contrite. 'I ought not to have let myself say that. It's only that I had rather expected—I mean, I naturally hoped . . .'

Here we go, Justus thought wearily. A woman always returns to that. The old marriage-go-round is still turning; sooner or later the wedding-horse comes back.

'There is love in marriage and love outside marriage,' he murmured. 'One has to make a distinction between the two.'

He was convinced that Isabel would never make one, but he was to learn too late that this was dangerously untrue.

Not that this was immediately apparent. Her reaction was what he had feared. 'Do you love me?' she demanded intensely.

Without looking at her, Justus murmured: 'I do.'

It was not quite a lie, he consoled himself, because at least at this moment he desired her, and desire is one element of love. But Isabel as usual disconcerted him. She stood up, letting her embroidery fall.

Her blue dressing-gown flew open—too harsh and bright

a blue for her. He saw with surprise that she was naked beneath it. Her eyes in her pale face blazed.

'Then prove it!' she commanded hoarsely.

Justus had no option but to obey. He knew a moment's sheer physical repugnance, but Isabel held out her arms. He was caught in the web she had been spinning.

He closed his eyes and concentrated on Isabel's charms.

When Justus awoke, it was daylight—the thin, pale greyness that comes before summer dawns. The sun was not up, but the eastern sky had brightness that promised to turn to colour and warmth. Already, although the window was only an oblong translucence, he could see that it was going to be a beautiful day.

Justus was sweating because he had had a nightmare in which the spider had trapped him in a corner and then sprung. He had retreated backwards to escape its powerful, bristling body, through the open drawing-room window, over the balcony and down . . . He woke with that terrifying sensation of having fallen which is allegedly due to a missed heart-beat, but which feels to anyone who has ever experienced it as though the hangman's trap-door has opened beneath his feet. And even now the monster was watching, waiting . . . gathering itself for a second, more successful spring. Its eyes were on him; it marked every movement. With a cry, Justus turned over and sat up.

Isabel Bishop, lying beside him, chuckled—a full, rich, bed-shaking sound. Justus reverted to the present situation, which was a nightmare of a wholly different kind.

'Sorry,' he apologized, 'I was dreaming.'

'You looked very funny,' Isabel said. Her voice was lazy and sated, like her body, which occupied far more than its fair share of the bed. Justus saw with horror that she was encroaching. She edged towards him even as she spoke.

He sat up abruptly and swung his feet to the floor. 'I must be going.'

Then he remembered the spider in his flat below.

He was caught between Isabel and the monster, both of whom regarded him as their prey. It came back to him that the female spider devoured her spouse after mating. He eyed Isabel uneasily.

Isabel was contemplating him without uneasiness. There was even a certain assurance in her gaze. She was no longer the suppliant; she was the commander; she had become the one who takes and not the one who begs. She would never again be just an over-large, gawky young woman, hopelessly unsure of herself. Instead, in later years, she would be called masterful, domineering, and expressions less flattering still. The discovery that Justus, like all men, was expendable had made her at once something more and something less. She was a personality that has acquired a new dimension and yet is no longer whole.

She had planned her revenge down to the last detail. Justus should be humiliated before her once and for all. Only so could she be sure of getting rid of him. His pride, of which he had in her opinion more than sufficient, was riding for a Lucifer-like fall.

She watched him get up and pull his dressing-gown around him, suppressing the thought that he looked pathetic like that. His morning stubble was decidedly unbecoming, and his flesh, though still firm, was abundant and layered with fat. He put out a podgy foot towards his slippers. Just so might a baby's toes grope. *Would* a baby's toes grope, Isabel assured herself, so strong was her maternal hope.

'Shall I come down with you?' she offered.

'Don't bother,' Justus said.

Isabel pouted, or tried to. 'Doesn't he want his Isabel, then?'

'No!' Justus said, controlling his violence.

'Naughty! Is he going to kill that great big spider himself?'

Justus did not answer, but Isabel was insensitive now that she had at last got her way. She rose, and Justus had leisure to admire her figure before it disappeared beneath the bright blue dressing-gown. Apart from that, he was already regretting his involvement with her. He said again, 'Don't bother to come down.'

'I couldn't sleep unless I did,' Isabel replied. She led the way downstairs—she, who had always followed. The tables were completely turned.

Justus made no attempt to reverse them, but outside his own flat he paused.

'There's no need for you to see me home, Isabel. I shall be perfectly all right by myself.'

Isabel was too unused to being escorted to get the sarcasm of his remark. Or perhaps she was too intent on securing his humiliation. She made straight for the drawing-room.

'I'll just satisfy myself that it's all your imagination.'

Justus felt a terrible foreboding and hung back. It was not his fault if Isabel insisted on being foolhardy, on putting her head into the lion's mouth or the spider's jaws. He half expected the brute to make a rush at her; it must be hungry by now; but when she unlocked the door and marched boldly into the drawing-room, no sight or sound suggested its presence there.

The sun was just rising above the rooftops and the drawing-room was flooded with light, yet it was cool from the air that had come in through the balcony window, which had been left open all night. The spider, of course, could have made its escape through the window, descending on a length of web as thick as cord. It might now be lurking in the garden. Or squatting malevolently under an armchair.

But Isabel, who did not believe in its existence, gazed round the room and saw no sign of it, and what the senses do not perceive nor the mind accept *is* non-existent. Reality is subjective, after all.

'You can come in now,' she called to Justus. 'Your nightmare has vanished with the dawn.' When he still hesitated, she called again, commanding: 'Come on in and see for yourself; the spider has gone.'

Justus took an agonized step forward. His instinct warned him that there was something sinister in the room—something connected somehow with Isabel Bishop, who had changed in a mysterious, subtle way. She seemed now to be larger than life, a taunting figure, a priestess waiting to sacrifice her victim at a rite. But where she led he could not refuse to follow; no 'heaven-sent excuse' could be manufactured to deliver him from his plight.

He entered the drawing-room. The breeze through the window blew freshly, spilling the petals of an overblown late rose in a vase. One of them hung, suspended by the web of an invisible spider. Was it possible that the monster could have shrunk to *that*? Justus looked around him fearfully. There were still places in the room where the giant spider might lie hid, pieces of furniture which he would have liked to peer behind but dared not, because of what might happen if he did.

'Well, Justus? Are you satisfied?'

Isabel Bishop was watching him from the door, surveying almost with distaste his incipient pot-belly and the ovoid rotundity of his form. Now that she had taken the decision to dispense with him, she was surprised how easy it had become. She was about to humiliate one whom, twelve hours ago, she believed she pined for, and she felt nothing. Her emotions were completely numb.

She watched Justus turn towards her and grin sheepishly —a travesty of the comic fat man's grin. Then, while his features were still moulded in it even though the expression in his eyes had altered, she stepped smartly backwards through the door, slammed it shut, turned the key, and locked her lover in.

She heard his fists pounding against it and his hoarse cry, 'Isabel! Let me out!'

'Later,' she called. 'When you've made friends with your giant spider.' She heard herself laugh as she spoke. He was like left-over food in a refrigerator: she had had all she wanted of him and the rest could wait. She would release him later, white and shaken, and look scornful as he hurried hang-dog out. He would never be able to hold up his head in her presence, and therefore he would avoid her. She even doubted if he would keep on his flat.

And then she heard a new sound and a cry of terror that was to haunt her for the rest of her life. It was a curious muffled rumble such as a creature with eight long legs might make if it were running. The sound came from the drawing-room.

Everyone was very kind to Isabel at the inquest, especially when she let it be known that she was expecting Justus's child. There was a general feeling that Ancorwen must have been a bit of a bounder to commit suicide and leave the girl like that. The more kindly disposed said he was obviously unbalanced to fling himself from a window and contrive to break his neck without even the explanation of a note or a lovers' quarrel. What kind of suicide was that? In the end, Isabel's story that he sleep-walked (and after all, his mistress should know) was accepted as the likeliest explanation, and an open verdict was returned.

Isabel Bishop sold up her flat (she said it had Memories) and withdrew to a midland town. She lives just outside Sheffield now, styles herself a widow, keeps a photograph of Justus on the mantelpiece, and devotes herself to the up-bringing of her boy. The child is normal in every respect, to her satisfaction, except perhaps for unusually hairy arms and legs. Isabel smiles and says it is because she was frightened by a spider. She has almost forgotten that this is the literal truth.

Exorcism

The apparition of Simon Snipe caused consternation to all who saw it, but to none more than to Benjamin Shrubsole, who had murdered Snipe some years previously.

Fittingly, Benjamin was the first to see it, and in no less a place than Simon's own old home.

It was a hot July night, with a hint of thunder. Benjamin woke from an uneasy sleep. There, standing at the foot of the bed, white, phosphorescent and transparent, was the figure of Simon Snipe. He was dressed in a shroud, which gave him the undignified appearance of a man awaiting a haircut. But there was nothing undignified about the slow raising of his right hand. He raised it until it pointed towards Shrubsole, who felt himself come out in a cold sweat.

Gingerly, for he did not wish to disturb his sleeping partner, he sat up in the conjugal bed, three-quarters of which was occupied by his wife Susannah, formerly Snipe, for he had married his victim's relict. He had also, since the Snipe house was comfortable and spacious, moved in to share it with her, together with the contents of Simon's excellent cellar, to whose after-effects he at first attributed the manifestation of their former owner's ghost.

'What do you want?' he demanded hoarsely.

'I want vengeance,' Simon said.

'And what good will vengeance do you?' Benjamin protested. 'Will it make you alive again?'

He was relieved when Simon shook his head mournfully, although he had anticipated this reply. The death certificate had stated positively that the cause of death was drowning; it was reassuring that so official a document did not lie.

'You got the better portion, Simon,' he encouraged. 'You don't want to bear a grudge. You ought to go on your way rejoicing that you've escaped from this vale of tears.'

This speech was delivered in the same hoarse whisper for fear lest Susannah might wake. She had married him in all innocence, although she had not grieved over-long for Snipe. She was a substantial, phlegmatic woman, devoted to food and drink. Only a starveling of Benjamin's meagre proportions could have found such satisfaction in bulk.

For Susannah had been the cause of his undoing. Unholy passion had burned in his breast. It was intolerable tha tall, stooping, cadaverous Snipe should have her and not realize what a treasure he had got.

'Eats enough for three,' Simon had moaned once in the bar of 'The Worrying Staghounds', 'and don't do the work of one. Women——!' He took a melancholy swallow and wiped the distasteful subject from his lips.

Remembering this, Benjamin did not hesitate to use it. 'It wasn't as if you loved Susannah,' he urged. 'You had a happy release and you went quickly. I held you under to make sure o' that.'

'That and other things,' Simon said succinctly. Benjamin did not bother to contradict. He had succeeded to Simon's wife, property, business, even his cellar. No action is disinterested.

'What's the point of wanting vengeance?' he persisted.

Simon indicated Susannah's recumbent form. 'I want you along o' me,' he insisted. 'Instead of along o' her.'

Benjamin patted Susannah's rump approvingly. 'I can understand how you feel. But her appetite hasn't diminished. She eats enough for four these days.'

'I don't want *her*. I just don't want you to have her.'

'Why, bless my soul!' Benjamin exclaimed, 'You're like a man with a peptic ulcer who expects everyone else to live on slops.'

'Who's talking about slops?'

'I was speaking metaphorically. What use is a great fleshly lump to you?'

He traced lovingly the billows in the bedclothes. Susannah stirred and moaned in her sleep. 'Will you be staying long?' he enquired anxiously. 'I think she's going to wake up.'

'No.' Simon shook his head and hurried on to the peroration which he had carefully prepared in advance. 'Wretch, you have robbed me of my life (Benjamin muttered, 'Prove it!') and for that yours is forfeit. Oh, be warned! Before the next full moon I will have vengeance.'

'Don't talk daft,' Benjamin said, 'it's already half way to the full. And there's nothing you can prove. Your death was accidental. You fell into a gravel-pit and drowned. If you don't believe me, I'll show you the report of the inquest. I always keep useful newspaper cuttings on file.'

'I wish you wouldn't interrupt,' Simon said crossly. 'I was warning you to be warned.' He raised his arms and said in awful accents: 'Shrubsole, prepare to meet thy G——'

There was a crash of thunder, the bed heaved, and Susannah woke, startled. The apparition had obligingly gone.

'You were talking in your sleep,' she accused her husband, who asked uneasily if she had heard what he said.

'No. Wasn't interested.' She threw an arm like a Doric column across him and rolled him over to her three-quarters of the bed.

Later in that same week of thundery weather, the apparition of Simon Snipe appeared to a certain Josiah Sledd. Josiah Sledd was a carpenter, and had buried Simon, since he carried on a small undertaking business on the side.

Sledd's first thought was that there must have been a flaw in the funeral arrangements; his second that Snipe had left it a bit late to complain; his third that it would in any case be impossible to make a refund so long after the bill had been paid.

This being so, he looked on Simon's ghost more favourably. 'Won't you come in?' he said.

'I *am* in,' Simon pointed out.

Sledd noted that this was true and also that all the doors were shut. He began to feel uneasy. 'What's disturbing your rest?' he enquired.

'Rest!' Simon protested. 'Is that what you call it? I was murdered, Josiah Sledd.'

Josiah's uneasiness increased considerably. 'You *were* out o' luck,' he said. 'I thought you fell into the gravel-pit while——' He had been going to say 'under the influence', but changed it to 'under the weather' instead.

'I was inveigled thither,' Simon announced, as if giving a recitation, 'and most foully done to death. Can you imagine yourself led out along that narrow landing-stage and, at the end of it, pushed in?'

'No,' Josiah said emphatically. 'But then, I'm not an imaginative man.'

He had been told this repeatedly since his schooldays, but

present events were beginning to make him doubt. Who but an imaginative man would fancy he saw in his workshop the ghost of one whom he had buried six feet deep? And claiming, moreover, to have been murdered? 'Who pushed you in?' he enquired.

'Ah,' Simon said, 'that would be telling.'

'Well, isn't that why you're here?'

'No, I've come to claim vengeance,' Simon informed him.

'You've left it long enough to claim.'

'What's the hurry? It ain't like the insurance.'

'No,' Josiah admitted, 'perhaps not. But it isn't going to do you any good, now is it? Why not let the sleeping dog lie?'

'Because he's lying in the wrong bed.'

'What's wrong with it?'

'It's double. And his ought to be as narrow as mine.'

Looking at Simon's tall, thin, stooping figure, Josiah reflected that this was pitching it pretty strong. 'You don't want to be like the dog in the manger,' he counselled. 'We're not all built the same.'

His own build was decidedly ample. No narrow bed would have suited him. He consoled himself with the thought that none was intended. *He* at least had not pushed Simon Snipe in.

The doleful event had taken place in the early hours of a New Year's morning, when Simon was assumed to have been staggering home from a social gathering in the bar of 'The Worrying Staghounds'. He had been found the following day, after Susannah, who had lethargically registered his absence, had informed the village P.C. The constable, a man unsuspicious by nature, had actually been taking a short cut, after a day of circuitous and fruitless enquiries, when he passed the old gravel-pit. The pit was wide and deep and a small landing-stage ran out towards the middle. Representations were occasionally made that it should be fenced, but it was pointed out that no one ever went there except when taking a short cut or a wrong turning—as had surely happened to Simon Snipe. However, the coroner at Snipe's inquest had seen fit to draw attention to the danger, and in due course a sign saying 'Danger' had accordingly been put up. Simon might thus be regarded as a public benefactor—a fact which Sledd did not hesitate to stress.

'You can be proud of what you did for the village, Simon,' he assured him. 'Men have got an O.B.E. for less.'

'Ay, but not an R.I.P.,' Simon objected.

'Must you keep on about it so?'

'I'll be as quiet as the grave once I've taken vengeance.'

'What exactly are you going to do?'

'I'm going to lead him to the gravel-pit.'

'Lead who?' Josiah interrupted.

'Him as led me,' Simon said. 'And then I'm going to push him in and hold him under long enough to be sure he's dead.'

Resolving never in any circumstances to go near the gravel-pit, Josiah made a last conciliatory attempt.

'I never thought to hear you utter such unchristian sentiments, Simon, when I buried you in six feet of clay.'

'Five and a half,' Simon corrected him. 'You gave short measure, Sledd.'

'It was extra long measure the other way,' Josiah justified. 'And the ground was hard with frost.'

'Not so hard as the heart of my murderer.'

'Maybe, but I didn't have to dig a hole in that.'

'You'll be digging a grave for him soon,' Simon promised. 'Before the new moon is full.'

Josiah had been thinking of taking a few days' holiday, but decided that, in view of prospective business, he would wait.

'I take that very kindly of you, Simon. Not everyone is thoughtful enough to have a long illness, or give advance notice, so to speak. Now if you could just indicate who it is so I can get the measurements—in the most tactful way, of course.'

Simon raised his arms. 'Beware!' he cried.

Outside the thunder muttered.

Simon reiterated the word 'beware'.

The muttering grew to a rumble and the rumble crashed mightily overhead. Josiah Sledd's attention was momentarily distracted. When it returned, the ghost of Simon Snipe had fled.

Simon appeared to several other people in the village. All the visitations followed the same pattern, more or less. Before long it came to the ears of Susannah Shrubsole that her late spouse was indelicately haunting the place.

'Simon never knew when he wasn't wanted,' she pronounced in an obituary-like tone. And added a moment later: 'Cheek I call it, seeing as I've married again.'

Benjamin agreed with her warmly. 'Can I tell him you said so?' he asked.

'If he hasn't got the courage to call in person. I've never given him cause to cut me dead.'

The expression struck Benjamin as infelicitous. Besides, he did not want Susannah to encounter Simon Snipe. There was no knowing how she might react to the apparition's accusations, let alone its demands for revenge. There had been a moment when Benjamin's blood had run as cold as Simon's on learning that Susannah had heard from Josiah Sledd (who might have minded his own business) a detailed, not to say decorated, version of what was alleged to have occurred. He had had a nasty minute wondering whether she might believe it, but it did not enter her head that it could be true. She attributed it entirely to Simon Snipe's malice, and was mildly flattered to arouse jealousy even in the tomb.

'Not that he wanted me much,' she said meaningly to his successor. 'You'd have thought he'd be glad to let me go.' She helped herself to another slice of treacle pudding. 'But he was always one for causing trouble. Only this time he's gone too far.'

'Hear, hear!' Benjamin agreed with fervour.

Susannah's mouth stopped working in mid-chew. 'Vengeance,' she mumbled, 'I'll give him vengeance.'

Her husband asked what she was going to do.

'I'm going to have him exorcized,' Susannah said firmly. 'That'll put paid to him. Getting out of his grave and traipsing round trying to make trouble! I'm going to go and see the Reverend Fibbs.'

She was as good as her word, though Benjamin was in two minds about it and begged her to consider the step first. If it worked, all well and good; but if it didn't . . . ? There was always the risk of bad becoming worse.

But Susannah was in no mood to consider his objections, any more than she had considered the accusations of Snipe. Husbands made difficulties and wives ignored them; experience had taught her that the wives were usually right.

So the Rev. Gervase Fibbs, a young and inexperienced

cleric, was somewhat taken aback to receive a visit from Mrs Shrubsole with the request that he exorcize her late husband's ghost. He temporized, and telephoned the Bishop, who thought the experiment should be circumspectly carried out, but with as few witnesses as possible—immediate relatives at most.

'Don't make any song and dance about it,' he counselled. 'If these things don't work they can have a boomerang effect—No, I do *not* mean on the person of the celebrant; I am speaking of the prestige of the Church. You tell me that the apparition has been widely witnessed, which means we can't afford a débâcle. The best thing would be to persuade Mrs Shrubsole to keep her mouth shut—that's only a suggestion, of course.—Yes, I quite agree the ceremony's archaic. It's a pity Mrs Shrubsole's one of ours. One always feels that the Church of Rome in these matters . . . No, I don't think Father O'Malley's œcumenically-minded—at least not œcumenically-minded enough for that.—I'm afraid I don't remember the details of the ceremony, but you ought to be able to arrange it pretty well. Personally, I've always thought the bell, book and candle business quite effective. I wish you the best of luck. Oh, and by the way, I'd be interested to know what happens—in strictest confidence, of course. We must see if we can arrange for you to dine at the Palace—my secretary will drop you a line . . . And now, if you'll excuse me, I've a Diocesan Board at eleven . . . What's that—my prayers? My dear fellow, of course, of course.'

There was thus no way out of what appeared to be a Christian duty. The Rev. Gervase Fibbs was depressed, weighed down in more senses than one by the items he carried in his briefcase on the afternoon he set out to exorcize

Simon Snipe. So far as he knew, there would be no one present but Susannah. Benjamin had refused to attend on the grounds that it would not be delicate in a second husband to be present at a ceremony so intimately connected with the first.

In fact, wild horses would not have secured his presence. He was not a superstitious man, but there were some things that even the most hardened sceptic balked at because they tempted providence too far. He had read that it used to be believed that a murdered man's wounds bled in the presence of his murderer, and had been glad that in Snipe's case there had been no blood. But to attempt to exorcize a murdered man's spirit in the presence of his murderer might produce a no less startling result.

He therefore announced his intention of being absent for the rest of the appointed day, and set off after lunch with no particular idea of where he was going, except that he intended to keep comfortably far away. It was early-closing day, which meant that the village was deserted. He did not encounter a soul—a desolation that would not normally have struck him, but which today seemed eerie and strange. Preoccupied with the afternoon's programme and his own reactions, he tramped stolidly and unheedingly on. It was all very well for Susannah to call in the aid of the vicar, but he was not sure that he agreed with it. Tampering with what you didn't understand was a dangerous business, even if you did wear your collar back to front. Suppose Simon's forces were stronger than the vicar's? Suppose the whole thing went wrong?

So deep in dark brooding was Benjamin that he failed to notice his direction until something familiar about the landscape pulled him up with a start. There was no doubt about where he was going; he was heading for the old gravel-pit.

His first thought was to retrace his footsteps: the spot seemed inappropriate this afternoon. His second was that this was a foolish reaction: if the place had associations these were about to be religiously charmed away. There was no reason in the world why he should not visit the gravel-pit; henceforth he could do so whenever he liked. And then for a long and dreadful minute his heart stopped beating, for there, leaning upon the sign marked 'Danger', was the ghost of Simon Snipe.

Unable to think of anything else to do, Benjamin greeted Simon politely, and the salutation was returned. Then, to his dismay, the ghost fell into step beside him, and his body and Simon's spirit walked on. Benjamin began to wonder if anything had gone wrong with the exorcism arrangements, for surely Simon should be at home, suffering the exhortations and conjurations of the Rev. Gervase Fibbs—who, as it happened, was at that moment shaking the creases out of his vestments in Susannah's dining-room.

Simon seemed quite unaware of any prior engagement.

'I didn't expect to see you here,' Benjamin said, hoping that this might jog his memory.

'I dare say you didn't,' Simon replied. He looked sideways at his companion and added: 'Remember the last time we walked along here?'

Benjamin was only too mindful of it, although the contrast could hardly have been more marked. Then there had been a sprinkling of snow on the ground and it was moonlight; whereas this afternoon the sky had a leaden look, as though some elemental unpleasantness were in the offing but had not yet declared itself, so that the cloud-curtains were carefully drawn to prevent the smallest whisper escaping which, by forewarning, might lessen the effect.

The stars had been bright on the night he murdered Simon. A high, small moon had illuminated the scene, silvering with frost the twigs and glinting on dark water, striping and chequering with black and white and silver the ruts and bents and all that lay between. Even Simon, not normally receptive to beauty, had glanced uneasily around.

'Are you certain this is the right road?' he had demanded.

Benjamin had assured him that it was.

When they reached the gravel-pit and the landing-stage, Simon said he was sure that it was not.

'It is,' Benjamin insisted, taking his arm and steering him towards the wooden planking.

With noisy truculence, Simon gave vent to his alarm.

'Hush,' Benjamin warned him. 'You'll fall in.'

And sure enough there was a mighty splash as Simon, for all his reluctance, contrived to take that extra pace over the edge. To Benjamin's disappointment, he came up for air and began swimming strongly, but he had envisaged such an event and had previously loosened a plank from the landing-stage. With this he was able to hold Simon down. The operation did not take long and he was home soon after midnight. The following day Simon's body had been found.

These recollections made it all the more disquieting to be accompanied on the present occasion by Simon's ghost.

'Oppressive weather,' Benjamin observed, unobtrusively loosening his collar.

Simon agreed that it was.

'Shouldn't be surprised if we had a thunderstorm,' Benjamin continued. 'I hope you won't get wet.'

He hoped the ghost might take the hint and withdraw to shelter, preferably the shelter of his home, where the exorcism rites must surely be proceeding. Instead Simon gave a short laugh. 'Not so wet as you'll be getting,' he promised his companion. 'You'll be like a drowned rat by and by.'

The simile struck Benjamin uncomfortably. 'What do you mean?' he enquired.

'I mean I'm going to drown you in the gravel-pit.'

'You can't do that!'

'Why not?'

'Well—why?' Benjamin countered. 'It would be pointless.'

'It would be for vengeance—like I said.'

'Look here, you're not still harping on what happened on our last visit here, are you? It's not like you to bear a grudge.'

It was in fact exactly like Simon to do so, which was what made Benjamin so ill at ease. He looked round, with an eye to making a break for it, but whichever way he turned, the ghost was there. It was as though Simon anticipated his movements, and although his transparent body did not block the view, Benjamin felt a certain hesitation about ignoring it; he could not decide whether it would be more frightening to pass through or not pass through.

Simon regarded him maliciously. 'I like to pay my debts.'

'Certainly, but I'm not charging you interest on this one. In fact, I'm prepared to write it off.'

There was a note of desperation in Benjamin's voice as he made this offer. Exorcism seemed singularly ineffective, although of course he could not know that the Rev. Gervase Fibbs had had some trouble lighting the candle and had then lost his place in the book. Susannah had set out the dining-room table with a lace tablecloth and a silver épergne. The effect at one end was altar-like, but the other end was laid for tea, and Mr Fibbs, who was the kind of bachelor who often goes hungry, felt his concentraton seriously impaired. With the best china, three sorts of cake and chocolate biscuits, it would be most unfortunate if anything untoward occurred.

He looked at Susannah to see how she was faring. 'If you're ready, Mrs Shrubsole, we'll begin.'

She indicated Simon's photograph, placed on the sideboard. 'It's not me you've got to get rid of, Vicar—it's him.'

Mr Fibbs glanced nervously at Simon, cleared his throat, and intoned, 'In the name of the Father, and of the Son . . .'

Benjamin Shrubsole also glanced nervously at Simon though for different reasons. Simon, normally only too anxious to drive home a bargain, was showing no inclination to write off his debt. Even more alarming was the fact that, willy-nilly, they had reached the gravel-pit.

Not a leaf moved, not a bird fluttered; the sky seemed to be holding its breath and at the same time closing in around them; the light was thickening and distance was blurred. The gravel-pit stood in the midst of nowhere, as though already it were in another world.

With Simon's ghost crowding behind him, Benjamin set one foot on the landing-stage. The planks rang hollowly, like a coffin. Instinctively Benjamin stepped back.

'What's the matter?' asked Simon's ghost at the level of his ear-hole.

'That landing-stage doesn't feel safe.'

'Safe as houses.' Simon walked rapidly to the end and returned as quickly. 'What could be safer than that?'

Benjamin forbore to point out that Simon's footsteps were noiseless; not even the grass had bent beneath his weight. Yet the presence of the ghost, again behind him, was compulsive. He was forced gradually along the landing-stage.

There was no wind, yet at his approach the water ruffled. It slapped the planks like a monster smacking its lips. There was a coldness at Benjamin's back that emanated from Simon —coldness at the back and the end of the landing-stage in front.

A plank moved underfoot and Benjamin staggered. He barely recovered himself in time.

'Careful,' he protested, turning to look at his companion. 'Remember I can't swim.'

'I know.'

It struck Benjamin that the plank must be the one he had loosened for the purpose of holding down the swimming Simon. In the circumstances his reminder had been tactless. 'I beg your pardon,' he said.

'What for?'

'For mentioning that plank. I'd—er—forgotten about it.'

'I hadn't,' Simon said.

There was an unrelenting quality about his voice and presence. He was clearly in an obstinate mood.

And no man could be more obstinate than Simon, as Susannah, his widow, knew well. She looked uneasily from his photograph to the vicar: suppose he were obstinate now? And he might well be; he had had little use for the clergy. It would be too embarrassing if he refused to leave; or rather, since his ghost was not actually present, if he reappeared later on.

She wished Mr Fibbs would not hurry his adjurations; he

was going at an almost indecent speed. Perhaps Simon would not hear what he was saying. She tried very hard to catch the vicar's eye.

Mr Fibbs tried equally hard not to catch Susannah's. He knew he was reading too fast, but the whole set-up angered and appalled him. He was very modern in his views. He struck the bell for the first time and it pinged smartly; it was the one which normally stood on his desk and signalled 'Enter' to those who knocked at the door of his study. He hoped it would be equally effective in dismissing the unwanted guest.

To Benjamin Shrubsole any means of dismissal would have been welcome, but the ghost came on apace. The coldness at his back was arctic. He turned, and met Simon Snipe face to face.

'Look here—' he made one last appeal to reason—'this isn't worth it. What's it going to do for you?'

'It will balance our books,' declared Simon.

'I've already offered to forget about the debt.'

Simon spat expertly into the lake, which showed no ripple.

Benjamin tried again. 'To think that you could be lying snug and peaceful, pushing up daisies as they say, and you want to come traipsing out to a god-forsaken spot like this gravel-pit when there's an almighty thunderstorm on the way.'

For an instant Simon Snipe was tempted. He made no immediate reply. For some reason the thought of home (he had grown so accustomed to his grave that he thought of it this way) began to seem attractive once again.

' 'Tisn't as if this spot had pleasant memories,' Benjamin urged him. (The Rev. Mr Fibbs paused long enough to draw breath.) 'If I was in your position I shouldn't want to come back here.'

'We'll have to see about that.'

Benjamin realized bitterly that he had again been tactless —and just when things were beginning to go well. 'Of course, there's no accounting for tastes,' he admitted, 'but you can't be getting much pleasure out of this.'

'It's not pleasure I seek—it's vengeance.'

'You want me as dead as yourself.'

'Yes, in a manner of speaking.'

'Ah well, if you're sure that's what you want . . . though personally, if any man had murdered me—' Benjamin paused to see how Simon was reacting—'the last thing I'd want would be to have him alongside me in the churchyard unto all eternity.'

Simon considered this prospect, for he knew Benjamin was speaking the truth. Tomorrow—or the next day if the body was slow in being discovered—Josiah Sledd would begin to dig. Susannah had reserved herself a plot beside Simon; when she remarried, room was made for Benjamin as well. The three of them would lie together till the Last Trump, like the three characters who compose Sartre's Hell.

Not that Simon thought of it in this way; he thought of his home, and never had it seemed more attractive. Several of the local worms had become quite tame. There was one in particular, who nestled in his left eye-socket, for whom he even had a pet name.

Meanwhile, two miles away as the crow flies, the Rev. Mr Fibbs for the second time struck his bell. Its sound was unmelodious and inappropriate. It seemed as though it must break the spell (if any had been cast) of the ritual formula, of which there was a page yet left to pronounce. Susannah, however, slipped in an amen with fervour, as she did whenever there was a pause. She kept her eyes tight shut and her hands clasped tight on her handbag, which was stuffed with as much of this world's goods as she could muster—after all, with the miserly Simon you could never tell, and she preferred to be armed against as many disasters as she could imagine, money being her first line of defence.

Her second husband, however, had no more defences left against the fate that was approaching him in the form of the ghost of her first. Only a couple of steps separated Benjamin from the lake's dark water, and Simon's ghost still blocked his line of retreat. True, the ghost had not actually advanced in the last few minutes; but this, Benjamin supposed, was because he was meanly spinning out the pleasure, as carefully as he had once spun out a drink.

Unable to look at the water, because if he did he might lose his balance, Benjamin fixed his eyes on Simon's face.

'Simon,' he began, 'you and I have known each other since boyhood. Tell me: have we ever got on?'

'No.'

'Then don't you think there's something to be said for staying separate, now that a break's been achieved? Don't undo the good work, Simon, I beg you. We're a great deal better off as we are.'

At that moment two things happened: the thunder gave a long, preliminary roll, and Mr Fibbs struck his bell for the third time and called for peace to be to Simon's uneasy soul. Susannah said amen with even greater fervour (she did not like thunderstorms); and Simon Snipe, like one who remembers an appointment, began apologetically to withdraw. Or rather, not so much to withdraw as to be drawn backwards.

To Benjamin he seemed to recede; yet there was nothing of surprise or protest about his expression; he seemed to be perfectly in control. Simon himself could not have explained it; he simply could not be bothered any more to exact a childish and ridiculous vengeance which would ensure him the company of a man he heartily disliked. Nor did he grudge Benjamin Susannah; after all, he did not want her any more, and his experience of her did not lead him to think she was likely to make a man permanently happy; let Benjamin make that discovery himself. Moreover, the thought of his grave had begun to seem undeniably attractive; he would be sheltered from the thunderstorm, and he had grown acclimatized to the clamminess of his clay surroundings; he even missed the familiar musty smell. He had been away too long, and, like a householder returning from holiday, he was anxious to make sure all was well. He had been a home bird all his life and in death he was no different. His speed, proportional to his will, increased, and he flashed past his old house on his way to the churchyard without so much as a thought or a glance.

Susannah glimpsed him passing the window, and called out, startled, 'There he goes!' which so alarmed the Rev. Gervase Fibbs that he turned too quickly, knocked over the épergne, and drenched the table-cloth, the carpet, and his clothes.

As for Benjamin, all he saw was that his retreat from the landing-stage was open. He hesitated a moment, fearing a trap; then, as the first drops fell, he began to run forward. He did not stop and he certainly did not look back.

The thunderstorm was the worst the village could remember. Lightning struck the church spire and the weather-vane was broken off; it was thrown derisively into the vicarage garden, which was thought to be a portent—no one knew of what.

In bed that night Benjamin and Susannah Shrubsole lay awake while she recounted to him the exorcizing of Simon Snipe, not without a few embroideries and additions, because the facts had been dull enough.

Benjamin, who had made it as far as the bar of 'The Worrying Staghounds', by which time he was soaked to the skin, had spent a considerable time there restoring his nerves and staving off the ill-effects of too much water; by the time he reached home he was mellow in the extreme. He listened placidly to Susannah's recital. She was delighted at the departure of 'that Snipe'.

'The cheek of it!' she expostulated, making the bed shake. 'Coming here and upsetting us all like that! Though why he should think he could get away with it I don't know.'

Benjamin murmured: 'You can get away with murder if you try.'